Freddie Stockdale was
in 1947 and read law a
with his wife in Chiswick, and has three sons by a previous marriage. He also farms in Lincolnshire; runs Pavilion Opera; and is the author of *The Opera Guide* and *Figaro Here, Figaro There*, a diary about presenting opera on the road. His first novel, *The Bridgwater Sale*, is also published by Black Swan.

Also by Freddie Stockdale

THE BRIDGWATER SALE

and published by Black Swan

Criminal Conversations

Freddie Stockdale

BLACK SWAN

CRIMINAL CONVERSATIONS
A BLACK SWAN BOOK: 0 552 99547 9

Originally published in Great Britain by Doubleday,
a division of Transworld Publishers Ltd

PRINTING HISTORY
Doubleday edition published 1994
Black Swan edition published 1995

Copyright © Freddie Stockdale 1994

The right of Freddie Stockdale to be identified as author of
this work has been asserted in accordance with sections
77 and 78 of the Copyright Designs and Patents Act 1988.

All of the characters in this book are fictitious, and any
resemblance to actual persons, living or dead, is purely
coincidental.

Conditions of sale

1. This book is sold subject to the condition that it
shall not, by way of trade or otherwise, be lent, re-sold,
hired out or otherwise circulated in any form of binding
or cover other than that in which it is published and
without a similar condition including this condition being
imposed on the subsequent purchaser.

2. This book is sold subject to the Standard Conditions of
Sale of Net Books and may not be re-sold in the UK below
the net price fixed by the publishers for the book.

Set in 11/12pt Linotype Melior by
Phoenix Typesetting, Ilkley, West Yorkshire.

Corgi Books are published by Transworld Publishers Ltd,
61–63 Uxbridge Road, Ealing, London W5 5SA,
in Australia by Transworld Publishers (Australia) Pty. Ltd,
15–25 Helles Avenue, Moorebank, NSW 2170,
and in New Zealand by Transworld Publishers (N.Z.) Ltd,
3 William Pickering Drive, Albany, Auckland.

Reproduced, printed and bound in Great Britain by
Cox & Wyman Ltd, Reading, Berks.

To Adele, with love

Chapter 1

'And then he struck you?'

'Yes, sir.'

'Several times?'

'Yes, sir.' The young woman pushed back her blonde curls and stared at the ceiling.

'On your bare bottom?'

'Well, it was nearly midnight.' There was a muffled snort from the jury box and the judge directed a stern glance towards the jurors.

'The Court is indifferent to the time of the day, Mrs Knox,' said the young solicitor quickly. 'I am simply trying to establish the precise details of the alleged offence.'

She smiled at him, running her tongue along an uneven row of teeth. Not for the first time, he found himself smiling back.

'Well, Mr Bryce?' The judge had large ears and a rather languid air, but his voice was incisive, impatient.

Tim Bryce's smile died away and he flicked over some notes to concentrate his thoughts. A tall man in his middle thirties, with curly black hair and an aggressive, intimidating chin, his eyes held a cautious, even troubled, look in repose. He turned back to the witness. 'Had you asked him to beat you?'

She frowned, considering the question carefully.

'Well, no.'

'But you didn't object?'

'No.'

The judge was staring at the girl with open-eyed concentration. Her pale freckled skin was in strong contrast to the deep shadows under her frowning green eyes. At most, she might be twenty-six.

'At no time?'

She paused before answering, and shot a swift look at the elderly man sitting in the dock. He appeared to be reading a small diary.

'You must answer Mr Bryce's question,' the judge said coldly. If he had hoped for a glance from her, he was disappointed.

'I'm thinking,' she said. This time her assailant looked up from his book and winked at her. He had a leathery complexion that gleamed beneath the thinning grizzled hair, and wrinkles round his temples.

'I am asking you whether you objected at any time to the defendant beating you,' Tim repeated.

'No,' she said at last. 'But I did tell him not to bite me.' She threw back her head and laughed. 'He's a terrible one with his teeth.'

This time there was audible giggling and the judge picked up his gavel and gave the block beneath it a blow that gave him evident satisfaction.

'That's all I wanted to know,' said Tim, sitting down, and the judge's eyes turned to a large man with crimson cheeks who had been doodling hieroglyphics during the previous exchange.

'Mr Gregory?' the Judge said.

The courtroom was high ceilinged, panelled in brown mahogany and embellished only by a massive coat of arms behind the judge's chair. Although it was June, lamps with tasselled green shades glowed here and there to supplement such daylight as filtered through the opaque skylights in the roof. The air was heavy with the heat of the city outside and one of the jurors, a small woman in a loose green dress, kept shaking her head to keep awake. The men around her were rapt.

'Thank you, your honour.' Mr Gregory, a tall untidy barrister, his greasy wig perched askew on his balding dome, rose slowly.

'Mrs Knox,' he said. 'You are a prostitute.'

'No, sir.'

'Oh dear me,' he said putting on a thick pair of spectacles the better to scrutinize her. 'I have evidently misunderstood your evidence. I thought you had told the Court that Colonel Chesterfield paid you for these services.'

'Certainly not!' The girl's face had become pinker, her voice less assured, with just a trace, now, of a Scottish accent.

'Let me refresh the Court's memory.' Mr Gregory the barrister smiled at her and received an answering glare.

'You are paid a monthly income of two thousand pounds from the Chesterfield Estates Company?'

'As a secretary,' she snapped.

'You occupy a three-bedroomed first-floor flat at twenty-four Scrymgeour Square, whose freehold is owned by the same company?'

'Yes, sir.'

'You pay no rent?'

'No, sir.'

'You say that you are employed as a – secretary?' The pause was nicely judged.

'Yes, sir.'

'Will you describe your duties to the Court?'

'Well . . .'

'Speak up, Mrs Knox. The jury is anxious to hear this.'

She glanced at Tim for support but he was carefully looking away. She licked her lips.

'I take dictation.'

'*Dictation*?' Those who knew Mr Gregory recognized the triumph in his voice, the chance to score deeper against an adversary. '*Dictation*? I've no doubt you do! But what kind, Mrs Knox? Of what kind? That is what we want to learn.'

By this time Tim was on his feet protesting and the judge leaned forward.

'Yes, I agree. Mr Gregory, I do not think the prosecution's case will be furthered by harrying the witness.'

'I am greatly obliged, your honour.' The barrister bowed low and turned again to the girl.

'Do your duties include sleeping with Colonel Chesterfield?'

'No, sir.' She spoke firmly, clearly.

'No? But you do sleep with him.'

'Yes, sir. From choice, not from duty.'

'And is it by choice that he beats you, beats you so severely that your neighbours summoned the police who had to break the door down because of your screams?'

'Yes, sir.' And then in a burst of confidence, 'You see, we didn't hear them knocking.'

'I imagine not,' said Mr Gregory drily, and picked up a blue folder.

'I have here the police doctor's report that has already been received in evidence.'

The judge nodded and made another note.

'You have heard his evidence. The fact is that

Colonel Chesterfield, a man who was providing you with income and benefits worth not less than thirty-five thousand pounds a year, was beating you so severely that your screams alarmed the whole neighbourhood.'

The girl shook her head defiantly.

'You may shake your head, madam, but what I say is true.'

If Mr Gregory had paused then, the case might have gone differently. But he was tired, and tormented by the first signs of a bout of summer flu, so he persisted:

'Isn't it?'

All eyes were turned towards her, and the silence in the tall room betrayed the presence of a solitary butterfly trapped against the glass of the cupola forty feet above their heads.

'No, sir.' She had recovered her poise and, raising her face to her tormentor, she said very clearly, 'It is *not* true.'

'Not true?' He rustled his papers. 'It is incontrovertibly proved by the evidence. Kindly explain to the ladies and gentlemen of the jury, who are hanging on your every word, why it is not true.'

'I can understand,' she said slowly, 'that the point would be lost upon you, Mr Gregory. But the jury,' she smiled shyly at them, 'will surely understand why a girl might cry out in the arms of her lover.'

Tim laughed out loud as furious hammering quelled the general murmurs of appreciation.

'You see,' he said, when it was his turn to sum up on behalf of the Colonel, his client, 'much emphasis has been placed on two points by the prosecution: first that Mrs Knox's real employment was to cater for my client's perverted tastes, at whatever risk to herself, and secondly that the spanking she so enjoyed,' the lady in the green dress looked up sharply, so he quickly readjusted the sentence, 'a practice of which you may well not approve but which is very commonplace, was in fact a vicious assault severe enough to be characterized as a crime. But employment is not a barrier against tenderness. Who can doubt, seeing and hearing Mrs Knox's evidence, that Colonel Chesterfield, a distinguished soldier, indeed a magistrate, has been fortunate enough to earn her love.

'But it is the second point that needs your most careful consideration. This is a criminal case. His honour will instruct you, I am sure, that if an act is unlawful, being a criminal act, it cannot be rendered lawful because the person to whose detriment it is done consents to it. For no person can license another to commit a crime. There are, however, many acts in themselves lawful which become unlawful only if they are done without the consent of the person affected. Striking another person repeatedly with a cane such as Exhibit A plainly falls into this latter category. But when it is done in the spirit of affection, in the heat of passion, with intention to give pleasure rather than to cause injury, whether done by the Colonel to Mrs Knox, or, as we have also heard, by Mrs Knox in turn to the Colonel, both freely consenting, surely it is not for the State to intervene and take upon itself the onerous duty of instructing us how to behave in the privacy of our bedrooms?

'It is this couple's misfortune that the Metropolitan Police, in their zeal, should have misinterpreted cries of pleasure for those of pain. It is your great responsibility not to turn misfortune into tragedy by convicting an elderly soldier, who has served his country well, of loving too enthusiastically for the prosecution's taste.'

'Thank you, Bryce.' The three of them were standing on the street corner, waiting for the Colonel's car. 'You did me proud.'

'It was Mrs Knox,' said Tim, smiling down at her. 'You were the perfect witness. Nice and restrained, but with a real kick in reserve when old Gregory went too far. It was lucky he didn't make too much of the hospital records. Ten stitches! I'd have gone for that. You just knocked the stuffing out of him.'

The Colonel looked away vaguely. 'Come along my dear,' he said, gesturing at a dark-grey Rolls Royce that had drawn up to the curb. They all shook hands and the Colonel helped the girl into the back and got in beside her.

Tim watched the car disappearing into the evening traffic, and then walked very slowly back into the Court building. On a bench in the echoing marble vestibule sat his senior partner, Henry Ruggles, thick-set, elderly, immaculately dressed, his bald head moist with sweat which he kept wiping away with a stained grey handkerchief. Tim sat down beside him and lit a cigarette.

'Christ!'

'Now what?' The senior partner was used to the young man's anxieties.

'That poor girl.'

'On thirty thousand a year?'

'Three thousand pounds a stitch! I could have got her that in compensation.'

'No, you couldn't. Not as a partner in our firm. Colonel Chesterfield is our biggest client. Fifty acres of central London. It pays my salary, and yours as well. And she looks as if she thrives on it.'

Tim shook his head, but more in anger than disagreement.

'Anyway, you did an excellent job in there. No barrister could have done better. I thought he'd be lucky to get off with a suspended sentence. Let's get back to the office. We need to talk about the Ingram Trust.'

Chapter 2

The offices of Ruggles, Cavendish & Bryce had gradually spread over the first floors of three adjoining buildings just off High Holborn. In the early days, when Tim's father had started the partnership with his friends Ruggles and Cavendish, the three had shared two battered attic rooms in Soho.

A reputation for working all hours, and the early departure of the too-scrupulous Cavendish in 1937, had earned them enough work during the war to migrate to the City where the big money was beginning to be made. But they had kept their original name. The well-connected Cavendish had brought them some good accounts, among them the Chesterfield estate and the Ingrams family, whose multiplying trusts justified the full-time attention of a whole department. If these grandees had noticed the departure of Mr Cavendish, they certainly hadn't acted on it, preferring perhaps the buccaneering spirit of his partners to his own morose rectitude. Nor had they lost by their loyalty to the firm. Robust investment and a firm hand with opponents, whether creditors or tenants, had vastly enriched the clients, and thus the partnership. And even with a staff of nearly forty, there remained just three partners: Henry Ruggles, his son Robin, and Tim Bryce.

'A famous victory! I can see it in your faces.' The younger Ruggles, as corpulent as his father but still enjoying a full head of red hair, came out of the lavatory as the other two emerged from the lift into their glittering hallway. The back offices might be spartan to the point of destitution, but the clients saw a suite of rooms done up like a Georgian country mansion, with gilt tables, hunting prints and heavy chintz-covered armchairs. 'It makes them feel at home,' the younger Ruggles had insisted, oblivious of his visitors' wry amusement at his expense.

'Yes,' his father now laughed. 'Tim earned his keep today.'

'Notorious rapist at large again, eh? Well done, thou good and faithful servant.' Tim winced as Robin Ruggles slapped him on the back.

'Could we have some tea and the drinks trolley in the conference room?' Henry Ruggles had turned aside to speak to a burly man in striped trousers who hurried through to greet them, and now bustled away again down the arched corridor.

On the table ready for them lay three identical beige files stamped with the name Ingram, and each with the number '47' stencilled in red ink. The Ingrams were Henry Ruggles' principal preoccupation: their money, their aspirations and their problems. He was secretary to their businesses, Trustee to their settlements and executor to their wills. He paid their school fees, their medical bills, their bookmakers, their divorced wives and their undertakers. A still vigorous man of seventy-six, he could be said to be the one fixed point in the shifting sands of the Ingram clan.

These Ingrams were that unusual phenomenon – an Irish Ascendancy family who had prospered in this century. By 1922 they were on their last legs, squatting in Castle Ingram and moving their epicentre from one room to another as the ceiling of each in turn collapsed, the rafters ceding defeat to the combined encroachment of damp, rot and deathwatch beetle. At night, young Tollemache Ingram used to listen to the steady ticking of his family's last retainers, as they ate their way faithfully and inexorably from east to west. But then one night he, his brother Hyacinth and his grandmother were interrupted in their evening meal by a polite request from the leader of the local Fenians (otherwise the village greengrocer) that they finish dinner on the lawn so as not to be put at risk by the firing of the Castle. It seemed a fitting end to the family fortunes to drink their last bottle of French champagne while the whole demesne was illuminated by the blazing inferno of their home.

'That's the first time I've felt warm this year,' announced Hyacinth, draining his wine and throwing his glass into the laurels. 'Hey! Is that Mrs O'Kelly carrying off the silver kettle?'

'It is not,' said his grandmother, without looking up. 'But I'll tell you what. I believe we'll get the Insurance.'

She was right. The Trustees, ancient cousins scattered in the north, had entirely forgotten to insure the building or its contents at all. No niceties of exclusion clauses applied. They therefore felt themselves personally obliged to compensate their collapsed wards, and old Mrs Ingram's imagination had been fully stretched by the list of contents, right down to the silver kettle, that were deemed to have burned or melted in the blaze. Hyacinth decamped with his share to try his chances in America, while old Mrs Ingram invested her and Tollemache's share in a small stock farm west of London.

By 1939, Hyacinth was a partner in the corporate finance house Beeston Lefevre on Wall Street, and Tollemache's farm had sprouted nearly two hundred suburban villas. In the meantime he had married a Miss Esmond of Mount Esmond. That was the part that had pleased his grandmother; the part that pleased him was that his mother-in-law, Sybil Loomis, was heiress to the Loomis jute fortune.

When Tollemache died, in 1956, he left to his Trustees an estate of fifteen million pounds, of which, by rapid last-minute negotiation, the majority was invested in land, thus attracting very substantial death duty exemption. He also left to their care five children, with instructions that one-fifth of his estate was to be handed to the offspring of each of his children when the latter died, and the shares of any that died without issue were to be distributed, as they died, in equal shares to all his descendants then living. (But in the meantime, the income of the estate was to be applied by his executors for the benefit of his descendants in their absolute discretion.) All of his five children were still alive, and the estate was now worth over fifty million pounds, with not one penny of capital distributed.

It was a source of considerable bitterness to Tollemache Ingram's children, now in their declining years, that they were still dependent upon Trustees (admittedly open-handed Trustees) for their daily needs, while their children would in due course become magnificently independent. Coping with this administration kept Henry Ruggles busy, and rich. Moreover, which matters more to some people, it gave him an extraordinary amount of power. His fellow executor, Major-General Desmond Morne, a retired

Irish soldier, never visited England and simply signed the papers sent to him without demur.

Although the millions had been left by one Ingram for the benefit of other Ingrams, namely his descendants, the decision as to what would be paid, and more especially what would not be paid, rested with Henry. It gave him a deliciously magnificent sense of superiority over these ostensibly much richer and grander clients that he could, with just a twitch on the thread of their income, bring them back into his fold. Nor did this sense of omnipotence lose anything by being practised so discreetly as to be outwardly invisible. In a very real way, he knew what it was to be a god, accepting with practised grace the little (and sometimes not so little) offerings placed by supplicants upon the altar of his beneficence. All the older Ingrams knew, though they would never have admitted it even amongst themselves, that the difference between 'The Trustees deeply regret . . .' and 'Our cheque is enclosed . . .' could be a sacrifice as simple as including Henry Ruggles in a fashionable lunch party. It was all a question of keeping in communion.

But the reason for the latest meeting was a new and equally encouraging development. Hyacinth Ingram recently had died unmarried in New York at the age of eighty-five, leaving an estate, according to his lawyers, of nearly seven million dollars to be distributed in some other complicated fashion among the beneficiaries. Henry had, of course, been named as Executor, along with a partner in Beeston Lefevre.

'This is all very satisfactory.' Robin Ruggles leant back in his chair, and sipped his tea with a contented smile. And the others knew what he meant. At the age of thirty, he was beginning to contemplate marriage.

And who better to provide him with all the delights of matrimony than Miss Laura Ingram, only child of Tollemache's youngest son, she being already the unchallengeable heiress to at least ten million inalienable pounds upon the future death of her father?

Tim had opened his file and was studying the contents – six pages of detailed notes faxed from the New York lawyers detailing investments, the incidence of State taxes, and an outline note on the provisions of the will.

'It's very complicated,' he said at last with a grin. 'And splendidly precise.'

Henry Ruggles sighed. 'What a pair they were for tying everything up. When I think of those two brothers! They had virtually nothing but their name.'

'Forty-four quarterings,' murmured Robin, conscious that Miss Laura would inherit these as well. His father glanced at Tim but the latter was back among the codicils, making occasional notes with a pencil.

'Any immediate action?' asked Henry.

Tim shook his head. 'No. We wait. They're going through the formalities. There was a small sum on deposit, so they're preparing stock transfers for the securities. Nothing controversial. He had sold his house, one of the last on Fifth Avenue by the way, when he moved out to Katonah.' He laid down his pencil. 'We wait.'

Robin stood up abruptly. 'Then I'm off.' The others looked up and he couldn't resist adding, 'As it happens I'm taking Laura to a film.' Raising a languid hand by way of a parting salute, he left the room.

His father finished his tea, gathered up his file and paused for a moment. 'Do we need to talk about Colonel Chesterfield's bill?' he said.

'What do you think?' Tim's mind was elsewhere.

'I think we should charge him ten thousand pounds, as anyone else would.'

'And risk offending him?'

'It's your money. You handled it alone.'

'It was a dirty business. But if he pays the money, I'll take it.'

'Ten thousand then.' The older man left, well satisfied.

Tim sighed, pushing away his scruples. This was how his father had taught him. Take the tricky ones, take the risks, and take the money. He had a good job, very highly paid, when most of his contemporaries, those that had jobs, were gloating at getting a quarter as much. He was good at what he did. He earned the rewards. He poured himself another glass of whisky.

Chapter 3

The next morning brought a visit of one of the firm's less fortunate clients. Dapper Gumby, a pale willowy man with wavy grey hair and a perpetual half smile, lay back in the deepest of the chintz-covered armchairs and lit a cigarette. His suit, a pale mohair with a blue weave, fitted him so beautifully that the girl at the desk wondered whether his fortunes might not be revived by a new career as a male model. Everyone in the office knew, from the precise gradations of Henry Ruggles' greetings, how each client's affairs stood. And Dapper's affairs stood very low indeed.

'My dear Dapper!' The senior partner walked straight past him with a cheery wave, which was returned with as little ceremony.

'Tim will see you in a minute,' he called over his shoulder. Dapper shrugged, idly picking up *The Field* and pretending to examine it while covertly appraising the girl. Was she worth laying? It was the sole criterion by which his life was ordered. There was no humbug about Dapper.

The girl looked up to find his yellow eyes boring into her. She gulped. 'Mr Bryce will see you now, Mr Gumby.' He rose languidly and walked down the corridor without a word.

'It's very serious, I'm afraid.' Tim was leafing through the papers, and making calculations on the margin of the blotter.

'Will nothing be salvaged?'

'Nothing.'

'Well, I can't say you didn't warn me.'

Dapper, in selling his house and its remaining land to a Panamanian manufacturer, had accepted payment in shares in the company which had almost immediately gone bankrupt. 'I should have taken the cash. Three million pounds!' He shook his head and laughed ruefully. 'I didn't even have the fun of spending it.'

'The immediate problem,' said Tim reluctantly, 'is your other debts. The bank is being very understanding and I talked to Sir Robert yesterday. But the security is gone.'

'Can I have some tea?'

'Of course,' Tim crossed to a telephone.

'Milk?'

'Lemon, please. No sugar.'

'What will the pictures fetch?'

'Garrisons estimate a clear two hundred thousand.'

'Well, that's a start.' Tim sat down again, encouraged.

'Up to a point.'

'I see.' Tim continued to look at his figures. 'How much did they advance you?'

'Ninety thousand.'

'Which you didn't pay into the bank?'

'Of course not.' Dapper laughed out loud at the thought.

There was a knock on the door and the office steward came in with a tray of tea. Tim listened as the other swallowed his tea and munched a biscuit decorated with pink-and-white icing. He had always been fond of the older man, despite or perhaps because of his buccaneering ways. 'They may freeze your account,' he said.

'I wouldn't blame them.'

'The branch manager is very anxious to arrange a meeting.'

'You go.'

Tim smiled. 'Thanks very much! What on earth can I say?'

'Isn't that what I pay you for?' As he said it, Dapper remembered the sheaf of unpaid legal accounts, and shook his head ruefully. 'You see what a pickle I'm in? But,' he added, as Tim had not responded, 'I do have a plan.' He poured himself another cup of tea, digging at the lemon with the tip of the spoon. 'I'm going to get married.'

'Congratulations!'

'Oh, she doesn't know it yet. A beautiful creature, all pink and gold. You'll love her.'

Tim grinned. 'And how will this help?'

'Because,' said Dapper, momentarily serious, 'she's got masses of money, of course. You probably know her, Laura Ingram?'

Tim bared his teeth. He knew the girl only too well. Beautiful she certainly was, and wilful with it. The only time he'd asked her out himself, to join a party he was taking to the Coliseum, simply as a gesture of kindness towards an apparently lonely young woman who had complained of being on her own in London, her answer had been an astonished and condescending refusal. The memory of her raised eyebrows and sarcastic drawl still rankled. Dapper was welcome to her, or Robin Ruggles could have her, for all he cared.

'Now where's that decanter of yours?' continued Dapper. 'It's after twelve. I need a drink.'

* * *

While the two men discussed her future, the object of so many men's aspirations was walking down Jermyn Street. It was hot and bright, and the street reverberated with the rattle of taxis trapped in the steaming traffic. Laura, her face all but obscured by a broad floppy hat, slipped down Duke Street and into a little restaurant with frosted glass windows. The air inside was deliciously cool.

'Is my father here yet?'

'No, Miss Ingram,' replied the head waiter. 'But if you want to sit down, your table is ready.' He led her around the crowded little tables laid out with white linen and silver and into a second smaller room with wooden partitions.

'A glass of champagne?'

'Yes, please.' Laura sat down and, opening her bag, took out a packet of cigarettes and a small gold lighter.

'I wish you wouldn't.'

She looked up to see a tall, cadaverous man, dressed incongruously in heavy tweeds, frowning down at her.

'Dad.' She stood up, pulled off her hat, and kissed him warmly on his cheek. '*Hello*!' she said, sniffing deeply. 'Who've you just been with?'

Max Ingram drew back and turned to the waiter who had followed him.

'Will you bring me some champagne?' he said sharply. 'With an ice bucket.'

'It's already on its way, sir,' the waiter replied.

'If you think,' said Laura with a smile, 'that you can buy my silence with Dom Perignon, you're mistaken. You bear the unmistakable traces of Eau de Paradis. Let me see.' She paused for dramatic effect. 'Mother only wears Chanel. Maria wears Diorissima. So this is someone new. What a complicated life you must lead!'

'No other daughter in England would talk to their father as you do. You're only twenty-two, what do you know of Eau de Paradis?'

'Well,' she said, her head on one side, 'it's the most expensive brand on the market, it only suits a certain type. Oh,' she paused, 'and Perky Metternich wears it.'

Her father turned impatiently to see if his drink was approaching.

'And I wish you wouldn't talk in that way,' he said, turning back. 'It's none of your business.'

'Like Dapper?' she asked slyly. Dapper Gumby, being known to have squandered his fortune, was perhaps in all London the man least in demand as a prospective son-in-law.

'It's about Dapper, as you call him, that I wanted to speak to you.'

'I rather thought it might be,' Laura said. Dapper's attentions towards her provided the single non-contentious topic of conversation between her parents.

'You realize he's practically bankrupt.'

'Robin says he's way past that.'

'Robin? Who's Robin?'

'Robin Ruggles.'

'God in heaven! Don't tell me you're friends with that greasy lump of red lard!'

'Dad, really. He's very sweet. He took me to *Wotan's Farewell* last night. We had a lovely evening.'

'Well, he shouldn't discuss his clients in public. Heaven knows what he says about us.'

'I expect he says we're very rich,' said Laura laughing, 'and very discontented. At least you are.'

'Well, are you surprised?' Max burst out. 'All those millions and I have to go cap in hand to Henry Ruggles to ask if I can afford to give my daughter lunch.'

'Robin told me they pay you a straight hundred and fifty thousand a year, just for spending money.'

For the first time her father's face softened as he laughed. 'It really is intolerable. Is there anything about my life you don't know?'

Laura took his hand and gave it a squeeze.

'You're looking very beautiful,' he said, gazing proudly at her soft even features, the curved mouth, the wide pale eyes, and the cascading golden hair.

'I'm going to have a nose job,' she said, examining the menu.

He pulled his hand back, and banged the table. 'I absolutely forbid it. Your nose is the best part of your features.'

'It's too long,' she said simply, looking down it with a critical squint.

'You're not serious, are you?' He took her hand back.

'Gazpacho,' she said, looking up at the waiter who had just reappeared. 'And lobster salad.'

Max Ingram turned reluctantly to the menu. 'Oh, I'll have the hors d'oeuvres,' he said, then raised a warning finger. 'But nothing out of a tin, mind you.' The waiter's face expressed outrage, decently veiled. 'And the lamb cutlets, well done, with mashed potato. Are you?'

'Am I what?'

'Serious about messing up your face.'

'Look, there's Perky! *What* a coincidence.'

Crossing the room towards them was a tall woman

with a pale complexion, short black hair and large, slightly slanted, eyes.

'Laura!' she cried out. 'How lovely to see you!'

The two women kissed without touching, their faces angled outwards in a caricature of affection.

'You ought to recognize my father,' said Laura. 'He's still wearing your scent.'

'Max, how are you?' said Perky imperturbably.

'Am I allowed a kiss too?' he asked.

'Oh yes,' cried Laura. 'Go on. No one'll notice.'

'You really are impossible,' said Max, and gently drew the older woman towards him and kissed her cheek with a tenderness so little concealed that even Colonel Chesterfield, three alcoves away and four dry martinis to the good, was able to announce that evening, 'Perky's caught a new one.'

'No!' His hostess, the redoubtable Lady Woodchester, leant forward and spilt some of her drink on the Monopoly board. 'Who?'

'Big dark chap. Dressed like a farmer.'

'Truly black?' said another man, turning from examining a picture.

'No, no. Keep calm, Jim. Nothing here for you. Some country cousin, I suppose, with more money than sense.'

'They say she always insists on a settlement first,' whispered Lady Woodchester.

'Then she must be worth it,' rejoined the other. 'Because she's beggared two men that I know of for certain.'

Chapter 4

Tim Bryce still kept the house in Chelsea which he had inherited when his father died. It was larger than he needed, but it was so full of memories, most of them happy, that he was reluctant to leave it with no better reason than that it seemed an absurd establishment for a law student. Fifteen years later, he was relieved that he had not succumbed to a temporary feeling of self-deprecation. It was here, when his mother had left them, that he and his father had carried on, each hiding the hurt from the other, each pretending that they were sufficient as a pair. A succession of young housekeepers had cooked and cleaned, and if sometimes at night Tim had reason to suspect other duties, he was careful never to show that he noticed.

After his father's death, his mother had written from Canada asking him to join her and her second family. He had replied affectionately but in the negative. He felt guilty about not wishing to see her again – it seemed unnatural, even cruel – yet that was how it was. In any case, the last housekeeper had stayed on, changing her allegiance cheerfully to her late employer's son. She had only left the year before when it became apparent to both of them that a marriage, for life, would not work. Tim had felt nothing as he watched her follow his mother's path away down the street. Perhaps my emotional life ended then, he thought. Perhaps I can never trust myself to care again. Or, more particularly, perhaps he dared not risk another rejection.

Now as he opened the door into the hallway, stooping to pick up the afternoon letters, he caught himself listening for sounds of the past, his father coughing in his upstairs study, or Jennie singing to herself in the kitchen. He poured himself a generous measure of whisky, and let himself out of the french windows into the large shady garden with its sweetly scented lime tree. He had hardly sat down when he heard the insistent summons of the telephone.

'Mr Bryce?'

He recognized the voice at once. 'Yes?'

'This is Flora Knox.'

'I know.' Why was he sounding so austere? His heart was thudding.

'Oh.' She paused, disconcerted. 'I wanted to thank you myself for what you did yesterday. It was very impressive.'

'How did you get my number?'

'It was in Colonel Chesterfield's Filofax.' Did she call him Colonel in bed?

'I see.' He could almost feel her uncertainty, but he could do nothing to help her. Yet he was thinking about her tongue, passing over her teeth. And about her body.

'Were you very shocked by the case?' Her voice sounded matter-of-fact now. Perhaps she was past showing vulnerability.

'Yes,' he said truthfully. 'I would much rather have been suing the Colonel for damages on your behalf.'

She chuckled. 'You don't know him very well.'

'Why do you say that?'

'Do you play tennis?'

'No.'

'Draughts?'

'No.'

'Scrabble, then?'

'No.'

'You're hopeless!' He could hear her laughing with frustration. And felt his own inhibitions melting in the warmth of her approach.

'But I'd love to take you out for dinner,' he said, sacrificing professional ethics in favour of human truth.

'That's more like it! Now?'

He felt unexpectedly breathless. 'Shall I come and collect you?'

There was a pause. 'No,' she said. 'I'll meet you, wherever.'

'Café Pelican?' He looked at his watch. 'Nine o'clock.'

'See you.' She rang off.

'I didn't beat you.'

'You didn't have to,' Flora murmured, shifting under his weight.

'Your scars have healed.' He nibbled at a convenient ear.

'Mmm.'

'What happened to Mr Knox?'

'He died.'

Tim opened his eyes, shocked. She was smiling crookedly up at him.

'He was terribly old,' she said, and bit him on the lip.

'I see!'

'No, you don't,' she said, still smiling. 'I must go in a minute. What are you doing with that?'

'What do you think?'

'I *see*!'

Half an hour later, he walked down to the corner of the street with her to hail a taxi. 'Please let me drive you home.'

'You can't,' she said. 'But thank you for offering.'

'The Colonel wouldn't like it?'

'Well – perhaps.'

'Doesn't like sharing you?'

'Would you?'

He moved away from her, feeling a tug of anger that threatened to intrude. 'It's none of my business.'

She took his hand. 'Thank you for dinner,' she said.

'Shall I see you soon?'

'I hope so.' As always when he didn't want one, a taxi was immediately at hand. She leapt in and pulled the door shut before he could claim a last kiss.

He shrugged to himself and turned away without waving.

Chapter 5

'Dear Henry, A farm on our eastern boundary is shortly to come on the market. It has 850 acres arable, with nearly 300 acres of woodland, and would very neatly round off the estate as well as vastly improve the shooting. It has a good period farmhouse and four farm cottages, all of which we would be able to sell off as our existing men can absorb the farmwork. In the present depressed state of the market, I think we could get it for under £2 million if we act swiftly, recouping a quarter of that from the surplus housing . . .'

Max Ingram laid down his pen angrily.

'I really think my father must have been mad,' he said aloud. His wife, engrossed in her book, did not reply.

'Why couldn't he just have given us the money, instead of tying it up in these ridiculous trusts? Amanda, are you listening to me?'

With a sigh, she laid her book down on the table beside her.

'Yes, Max,' she said calmly. 'I'm listening to you.'

'I mean, what can that idiot Henry Ruggles know about farming? Or about the economics of scale?'

'It seems to me,' she replied, 'that if the farm is

losing so much already, taking on more land will only increase the loss.'

'That,' he snapped, 'is because you don't understand the least thing about it.'

She picked up her book again.

'Don't you see?' He stood up in his agitation, and came over to tower above her, glaring down, his thick black eyebrows knotted together. 'We don't need any more men, or any more machinery, other than perhaps one of those wide-cut combines, and of course a bit of extra storage space. It makes such obvious sense.'

'What does?' Laura had come into the room and stood watching her parents, half sadly, half aggressively. Her father's menacing stance was becoming too much of a regular feature.

'Your father wants to buy the Griffins' farm. It's just come on the market.' Her mother turned back to her book with a shrug.

'It's none of your business,' Max snapped as Laura opened her mouth. 'Kindly leave me to make my own decisions.'

'It *is* my business if it involves the Trust capital,' she said smiling. She was well aware of her father's frustration when faced with the reality that he had never escaped his own father's control, exercised beyond the grave through the infuriating medium of Henry Ruggles. Although sympathetic, she was also aware that her father enjoyed a lavish income which in no way diminished her own eventual inheritance, and that this income provided him with an outward appearance of such financial stability that his bank were more than happy to fill in temporary gaps by extending him considerable loans, since he was always able to repay them in due course.

Max Ingram raised his arms and let them drop. 'Neither of you understands the thing at all,' he said, returning to sit at his desk. 'And Amanda, I wish you would keep out of it altogether. You only encourage Laura to be silly.'

Shaking off his daughter's hand, he stood up again and strode out of the room. Whistling for his dog, a curly haired spaniel with marmalade markings, he left the house and walked round by the stables and out through a wicket gate into the plantation of young larch trees drooping in the heat. With a wild yelp, the dog tore off into some bracken. A rabbit belted out the other side and dived down a hole by the fence.

'Here, boy, here!' Max undid his tie and opened his collar. The heat was heavy and the soporific sound of a pigeon calling soothed his angry thoughts. The Ingrams had been great landowners in County Mayo. Why shouldn't he work to re-establish them here, in Dorset? Work? This was the trouble. If he had a proper job, the income would simply evaporate in tax, added as it would be to the allowance Henry Ruggles sent him. He knew only too well that his occupation on the farm was not work. A local firm of estate agents ran the business, deferring to his whims and basing their fees on turnover rather than profit. The woods were sedulously kept tidy, with strips of kale and maize planted strategically along their borders to hold the autumn pheasants, every field was framed by dusty headlands, and the autumn ploughing uneconomically delayed for the partridges.

This had been his home for thirty years, shared for the last twenty-five with Amanda, brittle, self-opinionated, invulnerable Amanda. He kicked a lump of loose earth and muttered something.

Advancing years had not brought him peace of mind. He felt useless, dissatisfied, trapped. In a year he would be sixty, and yet, looking in the mirror, he knew he was still a vigorous, active, good-looking male. Why shouldn't he have fun? He could still beat Maria at tennis.

Maria! He clambered over the far fence and sat down under an old oak tree. He was conscious that he was behaving badly to Maria. At the beginning, eight, no ten years ago now, it had been exciting, those stolen afternoons, and then, when they grew careless from complacency, the occasional night in London, even a weekend in Strasbourg.

Then it had been she yielding to his frantic pleas, giving him a new sense of vitality, rejoicing that he depended on her. Was it just to spite her husband? If so, it had succeeded. The old boy had never really recovered. But latterly the dynamics of their relationship had shifted. Now it was she who pleaded, she who pressed him for insincere avowals, and lay awake while he pretended to sleep, gazing wistfully at the man she could no longer enthral.

Abruptly he stood up. 'I need to speak to her,' he said aloud, and by her, he meant Perky, as the thought of her lithe body, long, slim, intoxicatingly fragrant, sent him hurrying, almost running, back to the house. Secure in his office, he dialled her number.

'Yes.' Her voice sounded curt, businesslike.

'It's me.'

'And who's me?'

'Max.'

'You ought to be out enjoying the countryside.'

'I can only think of you.'

'Well, well,' she said. 'Thank you for the bracelet. It's very pretty.'

'Like you.' She did not reply. 'What are you doing?' he asked.

'Working.'

'On a day like this?'

'It's what I like doing,' she said. 'When shall I see you?'

'Tomorrow?'

'What time?'

'Eleven.'

'Eleven then.' She rang off, and the dialling tone was immediately interrupted by a second metallic click, the unmistakable sound of another receiver being replaced elsewhere in his house. He shrugged. Amanda's relentless spying was part of the cause of his disaffection.

Sitting at her desk, Perky pushed the emerald bracelet aside, and turned her attention again to the papers she was studying. Wrapped in a lemon-yellow kimono, her freshly washed hair tied up in a towel, she continued to add the right-hand column, pausing occasionally to convert the foreign currencies into sterling with the help of a small silver calculator. The final total was very satisfactory. With investment accounts in four countries, the freehold of her mews house in London, and now a small apartment block in Frankfurt, her personal demon, a terror of dependency on others, was beginning to subside.

She curled her long legs under the fragile chair and lit a cigarette. She was thirty-four years old; good for a few years yet, she decided with a rueful smile, judging by men's faces.

She had discovered her chosen career quite by chance, at the age of seventeen. She hadn't enjoyed teenage parties, being so much taller than the boys who approached her. Then, in a chilly house in Norfolk, her host had whisked her off for a walk in the moonlight. Even with a light frost, it was warmer outside than in. But he had insisted on wrapping her in his jacket as they meandered between the high hedges and came to rest on a narrow stone seat supported by crouching lions and covered by an arch of clipped yew. He had kissed her, shyly but with passion, and since she felt in the mood, she had responded enthusiastically.

Looking back, she supposed he must have been fifty, a stout man with kind eyes, who smelled of his pipe. In the distance the dance band was playing a polka. She had let him get as far as kissing her breasts before deciding she was hungry.

'I must go back.'

'Wait a moment,' he said, carefully replacing her clothing, and holding her tight against him. 'And think before you answer. What is there that you really want?'

A hot sausage? A glass of gin? She felt confused, vulnerable.

'You see,' he said giving her a companionable squeeze, 'what *I* really want is you. And because I'm lucky, I can perhaps give you something in return that you would really like. So think hard and don't be afraid.' Something in his voice made her hesitate, and then think.

'Ten thousand pounds,' she said, half inclined to giggle at the preposterous request. The man turned her so that he could see her face in the twilight.

'For one night?'

'Oh no,' she said. 'But for a start. To see how we get on.'

It had lasted five years by the end of which she had the lease of a flat in Kensington and enough invested to provide a modest income for life. Then came others, usually a year at a time; there had been no disasters and no great sorrows. If she had tired of the relationship, she simply raised the stakes until the man taught himself that possessing his money was more precious than possessing her. She, in turn, had come to value herself on a strictly commercial tariff. She had no friends, only admirers. Women watched her, half admiring, half afraid, from a healthy distance. She had never loved, not once.

Chapter 6

'Yours!'

Robin Ruggles scrambled despairingly towards the net and scooped up the ball only to see it smashed past his head.

'Game set and match!' shouted his opponents in unison, and he heard the thud as his partner slammed his racquet angrily on to the grass. There was scattered clapping from the onlookers, a couple on a rustic bench, his father in a striped deck chair and Laura squatting on a tartan rug.

'Can I get you a drink?' Robin said collapsing on the grass next to her. He wiped his face with his arm, trying to smile as if he was indifferent to losing.

'No,' she said. 'But I'll get you one. Pimms? Or Coke?'

'Pimms please. With lots of borage.'

She ran off, lifting her heels with enviable ease.

'I don't know what you pay that coach for,' grumbled his partner as he came up. 'You're as slow as a steamroller.'

'What about that lob?' Robin snapped. 'Ever tried wearing glasses?'

'It's only a game,' said his father seriously. 'You boys shouldn't get so worked up. It's undignified.'

'It's only a joke, Father,' said Robin in disgust. His partner walked away, and threw himself down by the bench. 'By the way, Laura was asking what you're going to say to her father about the land he wants to buy.'

Henry Ruggles looked round to make sure no-one was in earshot. 'You know we shouldn't really discuss her father's affairs with her.'

'I know. But in the circumstances . . .'

'Yes.' His father nodded. 'Of course, I've written to say that the Trustees don't feel able to invest further in land at the moment.'

'Poor General Morne. The things you do in the name of your fellow Trustee.'

'Well, he's only got himself to blame. I wish he would involve himself more. It would take some of the heat off me.'

Robin chuckled. 'You know you'd hate him to interfere. You love taking the decisions.'

His father nodded with an answering grin. 'Perhaps I do.'

'There's no perhaps about it.'

Laura came running back, and handed Robin the glass, slopping the russet liquid a little as she did.

He drank noisily. 'Oh-h! That is nectar!'

'I'm glad I give satisfaction.'

His eyes focused on her and she met his look with complete indifference.

'If you want another set,' she said, 'I'll play.'

'I couldn't,' he said. 'I'm worn out.'

'A swim then?'

'Let's.' He tried to take her hand but she was off again, scampering across the lawn to change. Henry Ruggles watched his son follow her with a wry expression.

Later, when their guests had left, the two solicitors, father and son, settled down in a square room with walls lined with books. One of the cupboard doors beneath the bookshelves lay open, revealing a complicated metal safe within. They sat face to face across a broad plain table, furnished only with a tray of pens, a computer terminal and a sheaf of paper.

'Mr Gregory's clerk is pressing for his money for that paternity case we used him for.'

'So?' Henry Ruggles had a small mouth with thin dry lips. He felt nothing but contempt for the barrister who had prosecuted Colonel Chesterfield. Who knew what might have happened if the disreputable old soldier had found himself facing six months inside? They might have lost one of their major clients. Let Gregory whistle for his money! It was, for Henry, one of the delightful features of the law, that while eloquent barristers might enjoy the limelight, the purse-strings remained securely under the control of their employing solicitors.

'Well – it is a year old.'

'He shouldn't go on to prosecute our clients then.'

'I don't suppose he can pick and choose. He's good. We might need him ourselves next time.'

The older man shrugged, then said, 'We're going to need someone pretty soon.'

'Oh?'

'Perry's Bank are bound to sue Gumby. But they won't want bankruptcy. They believe there are other assets concealed.'

'Tim's handling that?'

'Yes. He came to see me about it. He thinks it can't go on much longer.'

'We've never had an insolvency client before.'

'He wants to marry Laura.'

'What?' Robin leapt up, catching his chair as it fell. 'He can't.'

'She won't marry you.'

Robin glared at his father. 'That's all you know.'

'It's enough. Now sit down and control yourself. I've seen a lot of young women, more than you'd think. I'm sorry if it hurts you, but it's better that I tell you, and you face up to it. She won't marry you.'

'I love her.'

'I'm sure you do.' The older man rose now, and walked to the window. 'She's a pretty creature. But to marry a woman who doesn't love you, that's a real taste of hell.'

'My mother loved you.'

'Yes – and I loved her. But when you reach my age, you'll have seen what I've seen. Just put the idea right out of your mind.' He turned back, watching his son sadly. 'If it's any consolation, I've no reason to believe she loves Gumby either. Perhaps she's too young to love anyone. She amuses herself.' Robin shook his head, remaining silent. 'Well, perhaps that's not fair. But we *must* use this evening on practical matters. Gumby owes us nearly thirty thousand in legal fees. We could advance him some more, of course, but to what end? I don't see any prospect for him, nor does Tim. If the bank does sue, we must get our bills paid first and let them pick over the corpse.'

'Quite,' Robin said. They sat in silent agreement on this, at least.

'There's another problem.' Henry Ruggles turned on the computer and pressed some keys, putting on his spectacles to examine the display with care.

'Ten of the tenants in Chesterfield Square are taking legal advice about their leases.'

'Do we know who from?'

'Gallowglass.'

'Oh?'

'Well, they're entitled to enquire. But the Colonel wants us to be firm.'

'Meaning?'

'Eviction.'

'Can we do it?'

'Technically, we might. They've been withholding rent for repairs and disturbance. But two of them are on rather unusual leases, drawn up before our time. As the wording stands, the repairs are a warranty, whereas the payment of rent is a fundamental condition of the contract. It might succeed.'

'So what's stopping us throwing them out?'

'Well,' Henry Ruggles pressed another key. 'It's a little awkward. One of them is old Mrs Lubbock.'

'The Minister's mother?'

'Precisely. And she's lost both legs.'

'And the other?'

'Gwendolyn Ingram.'

'Laura's aunt?'

Henry Ruggles crossed to another cupboard and returned with a bottle of sherry and two glasses.

'Have you talked about that to the Colonel?' Robin asked.

'Oh no.' There was a pause as Henry poured out two glasses and passed one across the table. 'It wouldn't influence him. He hasn't involved himself in the detail, only the outline, of which he has an impressive grasp.'

'Could we plead conflict of interest?' It was every lawyer's worst nightmare – a major dispute between his two best clients, both of whom would naturally expect his vigorous and undivided support.

'Not if we want to keep his business.'

'This is good.'

'Thank you. It's an Oloroso direct from Jerez.'
'So what do we do?'
'I'm not sure. Think about it tonight, and we'll talk to Tim tomorrow.'

Outside, in the silent garden, the summer shadows lengthened on the deserted lawn, slowly encroaching on an abandoned tennis racquet and a pair of swimming trunks left out to dry. The red walls of the fat suburban villa grew darker and somewhere, in the roof above the two silent men, bats began to stir.

After his son had gone upstairs, Henry Ruggles carefully locked the door and then unlocked the bottom drawer of his desk. He took out a thick sheaf of papers, and spread them across the round table in the bow window. They were architect's drawings, very detailed, on shiny half-transparent paper that rustled luxuriously as he turned from one design to the next. For half an hour he indulged himself, examining the new revisions and in one case taking out a ruler to check a measurement. Then, hearing sounds of dinner being prepared, he locked them carefully away and walked down to the cellar to choose a bottle to share with his son.

Chapter 7

'Now! Now! *Harder!*'

Flora Knox, crushed beneath the flailing weight of her employer, valiantly tried to strike him a backhanded blow with the wicked little cane.

'I'll have to bite you,' he gasped.

'No!' she screamed. '*No!*'

He gave a grunt and collapsed on to her just as someone started banging on the ceiling below with what sounded like a frying pan.

What a way to earn a living! She lay back, not that she had any choice, drenched with his sweat, one leg crushed at an agonizing angle. Typist? She couldn't master shorthand. Catering? No-one had ever asked her to cook them a meal twice. Flower arranging? She giggled.

'Like that, did you, you slut!' The Colonel regarded her with one goggling complacent eye. 'Haven't lost my touch, eh?' His nose was running, so she looked away, feigning exhaustion. Pray Heaven he would go to sleep if the people downstairs would only shut up. A monumental snore reassured her. The pain in her leg was as nothing compared with the threat of further endearments.

Bedding Tim Bryce had been a happy inspiration. She had quite forgotten what fun it could be. Fingering the Colonel's flaccid flesh that afternoon, it had been Tim's face, Tim's firm torso, that had dominated her thoughts. It had been quite a risk, jeopardizing her job, and perhaps even his, for an evening of sexual fulfilment. But watching him in court, with his easy mastery and relaxed authority, she had found herself physically embarrassed by the need to have him. As she watched him crossing and re-crossing the courtroom, she became obsessed with imagining what lay beneath the black camouflage of his clothing and what it would be like to be buffeted by his embrace. And for once, she felt that the portrait of her presented in court might be of help in bringing him into her arms.

Despite what everyone must have thought, this wasn't her sort of line at all. It had all been the fault of a silly joke – answering an advertisement in *The Times* for a young governess. She had gone to the interview for a dare, and really, the Colonel had been so charming, and his offer so alluring, considering her debts, that she had submitted. That was nine months ago. But her debts were paid now, and she was beginning to rebel. What would they say back in Tomintoul?

She nearly laughed, then stopped, horror-struck at the thought of waking the sleeping man slumped across her. Her parents would be appalled. They were pretty startled when she upped and married old Mr Knox. He had taken some fishing on the Spey, fallen in and come to the surgery where she had a temporary job as receptionist. He had nice manners, a shiny Jaguar, and started sending her flowers. She'd been so surprised when, inviting her out to dinner, he had stopped the car in the forestry, whipped out some caviare and a bottle of champagne, and proceeded to take her with such tenderness that she had decided to accept him forthwith. A couple of wrestling bouts with one of the local young farmers had not prepared her for a considerate lover.

Poor Mr Knox had died of a stroke within three years, and another three had seen the end of his money, and a bit more besides. London was expensive compared to Tomintoul. She had written home encouraging lies from time to time and her father, who kept the Waddington Arms, sent her a reply and some chocolates every Christmas, her mother having never learned to write.

By their standards she was now rich. And by the same standards, she was utterly disgraced. But what else could she do? It wasn't a bad life, considering. A comfortable flat, plenty of money, and half an hour of hell once a week. There must be many others worse off. Thank God he wasn't younger! It was funny to think of him owning all the houses round about. Whole streets of them. More than all Tomintoul.

Wriggling slightly, she propped herself up on her pillow and moved his head so that it lay cradled on her chest, stroking his hair as she did so. He seemed much less frightening now. It was only when he was looming over her, shouting and hurting her, that she hated him. At other times, like now, warmed by the contact, she could feel pity, sympathy and even affection for the man who tormented her and supported her. It must be difficult being old, with joints that creaked and instincts that could be appeased only by disturbing your neighbours.

There was silence from downstairs. Really, they should be used to it by now. She never heard anything from them. Did they make love in grim silence, icily determined that no-one should hear? She had passed them once or twice in the entrance hall, a middle-aged couple, as thin as sticks, the man always staring at her, while the woman looked away. She had winked at him once, but he too had looked away. It must be nearly teatime.

'Thank you my dear.' The Colonel was awake. 'I enjoyed that, did you?'

'Yes thank you,' she said. He had asked her to call him Charles but she really couldn't manage it.

'I thought so.' He looked smug.

'Shall I get you a drink?' That way she might get him off her leg before gangrene set in.

'Yes please.' He rolled over with a contented sigh and wiped his face on her pillow.

She tried to stand but sat down again, pretending to look for something on the floor.

'Lost something?'

'Just my panties.'

'You won't need those,' he said, pinching her roguishly. 'I don't have to go out till eight.'

She poured three inches of malt whisky into the glass and splashed a little soda from the syphon. That ought to fix him, she thought. The paleness of the liquor disguised its strength and the Colonel was too thirsty to protest. He drank it in one gulp and lay back, signalling that he wanted to caress her. Counterfeiting a smile, she bent down over him, responding as she knew he required. Within a short while he was again asleep.

Chapter 8

'More coffee?'

Tim was sitting in the Chairman's room of Perry's Bank, a large eighteenth-century merchant prince's townhouse off Threadneedle Street that had long since been gutted to be fitted up with open plan offices around a tall bejungled atrium. Only this one room, richly frescoed with scenes of Eastern gaiety, remained of the original interior.

'No thank you, Sir Robert.' His eyes strayed back to the pile of papers in front of him. He would just have to be patient, he knew. He was the supplicant.

'It's a funny thing,' said the old banker, tipping back in his chair, and playing with his monocle as if auditioning for a part in a *Punch* cartoon, 'we've had the Gumby account since we first opened our doors. Sixteen fifty-three, you know. Those were troublesome times. This young man's father was something of a friend of mine. He was a Glazier, of course.'

Tim nodded, feigning bright-eyed interest. He was half-expecting to be offered snuff.

'Oh yes.' The banker mused on, 'He would have been Master in, oh, I think . . .' He paused to examine the dusty archives of his brain. In vain. 'Now,' he said abruptly, dropping the monocle, and leaning forward towards Tim, his pale eyes suddenly focused, 'it's not on, is it?'

Tim flicked through the pages. 'His overdraft is £724,340,' he read.

'With quarterly interest due next week,' prompted the Chairman.

'Secured against the proceeds of the sale.'

'Yes,' sighed the banker. 'Except he isn't going to get paid.'

'Well,' said Tim, 'he was paid, and the consideration was quite properly despatched here to you. What is unfortunate is that the payment was in non-voting Preference Shares in Sarti Consolidated, which have been suspended, as we know.'

So many of Dapper's problems had been caused by himself that it was ironical that this, his greatest disaster, had really been bad luck. He had inherited the great house and nearly eight thousand acres amid a positive fanfare of publicity at the age of fifteen when his father's car had gone over a cliff in the South of France. That was the (financially) good news; the bad news was that the land was heavily mortgaged, the house lay partly derelict, and the better contents had long since gone to pay for his father's gambling.

A different character could even then have restored the situation with care and economy. Dapper, however, was constitutionally disinclined towards anything resembling thrift. As soon as he came of age at twenty-one, the house was redecorated in the latest style, two-thirds of the estate was sold off to its tenants to provide some cash, and the rest was devoted to the care and multiplication of pheasants. Even this might have been managed had he not also inherited his father's taste for baccarat.

His final decision to sell all that remained, though sad, was at last inevitable. The price offered by

Mr Sarti was a good one, and would have left him still a rich man. When Mr Sarti had, at the last moment, offered to pay a rather higher price in company stock (ostensibly to profit both parties), Tim had strongly advised Dapper to hold out for the cash. His advice had been ignored, but on the reasonable grounds that Sarti Consolidated had just turned in audited profits of nearly a billion dollars.

Within six days of the shares being triumphantly deposited with Perry's Bank, Sarti himself was dead and the shares, after immediate suspension on the Stock Exchange, were seen to be worthless. The old banker sighed and nibbled at a Bath Oliver biscuit.

'It means he isn't going to be paid,' he repeated drearily. 'Since title to the house and land presumably passed on the due date' – he paused and peered over his spectacles at Tim who nodded without looking up – 'there will also be a considerable Capital Gains Tax liability?'

This time Tim did look up. 'Yes,' he said. 'Ridiculous as it seems, we think that too. Not on the house, of course, which was always accepted as his principal residence for tax purposes, but on the land. There will be tax payable on the notional profit within the contract price, regardless of the subsequent collapse of its component securities. Although it won't come to the Revenue's attention until his next tax return. It seems absurdly unfair, but as we both know, the law pays no regard to fairness.'

The old banker shrugged. 'So if we want our money, or what we can get of it, we had better bankrupt him now, before the Inland Revenue sneak in to muscle ahead of us in the queue.'

'I see the point,' conceded Tim.

The other man chuckled. 'I rather think you do!'

he said. 'It's written in block capitals. When's the contents sale money due?'

'Ah,' said Tim, burying himself in his papers. 'He's dealing with that himself. Next week perhaps?'

'Did you know,' enquired the banker in an artificially even tone, 'that a considerable proportion, nearly one hundred thousand pounds, was advanced to him ten days ago? The cheque, in case you are wondering how I know, was presented here yesterday morning through the Mount Street Casino who also bank with us. That is why I telephoned you this morning for this meeting.'

Tim's face expressed nothing but sceptical surprise. 'Well,' he said. 'Not knowing the full facts, I can't comment. But I don't think the contents were pledged to you in any way, were they?'

'Read this.' Sir Robert passed a single sheet across the table. It was, as Tim anticipated, a comprehensive personal guarantee specifically mentioning his chattels, signed by Dapper and dated late December the previous year.

'Hmm,' Tim said. 'I don't think this came through my office.'

It was Sir Robert's turn to examine his papers. 'No,' he said casually, 'we just asked him to sign it as an extra precaution.'

'Did you explain its significance?'

'Of course.'

'I would have strongly advised him against signing it.'

'We couldn't have continued to meet his cheques without it.'

'Well, Sir Robert, I don't think you and I need to worry over the past, it's the future that matters for our mutual client.'

The banker pressed a concealed bell button with his knee and the door opened.

'Ah, Gilles. Come in. This is Tim Bryce. Gilles de Wirth. I don't think you two have met. Gilles watches things here for our masters in Geneva. As you know, we have a majority shareholder these days.'

The two younger men shook hands.

'We'll give him forty-eight hours,' continued the old banker, still smiling as if continuing the introductions. 'If a hundred thousand pounds is paid in, we will delay bankruptcy proceedings for one month to give him time to call on any generous friends he may have. Failing that, we will institute an immediate prosecution for Fraudulent Conversion, with a matching civil action for the balance of the overdraft.'

'But . . .' Tim's mouth had fallen open.

'It might be prudent,' the younger banker spoke for the first time, in a voice that hovered between the genial and the sarcastic, 'for your firm to advance him the money. If we have to go for a criminal prosecution, it may not reflect well on his legal advisers.'

Tim managed to match their smiles. 'You've given me a lot to think about,' he said. 'It's an interesting situation.'

'They said *what*?'

The Ruggles family, father and son, sat staring at him from across the conference table.

'I know,' said Tim. 'I'm not seriously suggesting that we should.'

'A hundred thousand pounds!' Robin stood up in his agitation, pulling up his trousers, the belt of which had somehow slipped beneath his incipient paunch. 'What does he owe us already?'

Tim checked the computer sheet he had called for before joining them. 'Thirty-seven thousand, just over, plus VAT.'

'I'll go and draft a bankruptcy petition now!' was the reply. 'That'll get us in before the bank.'

'Now hold on,' said his father, whose face had been revealing a series of conflicting emotions. 'We can't do that.'

'Why not?' demanded his son aggressively.

'Because I happened to meet Dapper coming out of Boodles this morning and he told me he was lunching with Laura. The whole situation could have materially changed by now.'

Robin sat down again so hard that the chair cracked.

'Now look what you've done,' said his father gently. 'You paid a lot of money for those.'

'It'll mend,' snarled Robin, pushing the wreck away and pulling up another. 'She'll never take him. And,' he added, 'she's meeting me after six to go to an exhibition.'

Henry Ruggles shrugged. 'We'll wait and see,' he said. 'Now Tim,' visibly asserting himself, though more for his son's sake than his partner's, 'try to get hold of Dapper. I think they're lunching at Wilton's. Explain the situation. Try to get some sense out of him. Report back to me here at seven before I go home.' With that he rose and left before he could be contradicted.

The two younger men were left staring at each other.

'Whisky?'

Tim accepted gladly and fielded the decanter that was shoved at him, scratching the table as it slid.

'I can't wait to see that slimy bastard off our books

and into a cardboard box at Blackfriars where he belongs,' was Robin's next contribution. 'Soda?'

'No thanks. You can't mean that.'

'Him and Laura! That's a laugh. He must be fifteen years older than she is. I suppose she's flattered by being seen about with an old rake.'

'She could certainly afford to set him right.'

'She is going,' said Robin with savage certainty, 'to marry me.' And he walked out of the room, slamming the door.

'Good luck to them!' Tim shook his head at the memory of Laura's impish arrogance and gulped down the whisky in his glass. It had a reassuring tang, a familiarity that calmed something within him. Reaching for the decanter, he poured out a little more.

Chapter 9

Laura meanwhile had spent the morning scrubbing her flat. Her Aunt Gwen, Max's eldest sister, was coming for dinner and that always signalled a major spring clean. She got out of bed, made herself a cup of tea, and tuned in to the local radio network. It broadcast a continuous supply of pop music interspersed with undemanding chat show material, nothing memorable, nothing disturbing, just comfortable mush. Then, wrapped in pink cotton overalls, and armoured by thick yellow rubber gloves, she started. First the kitchen floor, then the bathrooms, then the cupboards. At ten she stopped and made herself a large pot of coffee which she drank, accompanied by a hot croissant, while reading yesterday's paper. Then back into the little dining room, her bedroom and the spare room, and finally, a quick dust round the wide sitting room, with its three tall windows overlooking the cherry trees in the square. When she had finished, she looked at her watch.

'Oh God!' It was after half past twelve, and she was due to meet Dapper for lunch at one. She ran back into her bathroom, spinning on both taps and squirting a frantic jet of verbena-scented foam into the water. Brushing her teeth with one hand, she began to dig bits and pieces out of her make-up box with the other. A quick plunge, a dash of shampoo, a burst of hot air, some fumbling with buttons and she was in her car accelerating through the squares towards Piccadilly.

'I'm sorry I'm so late.'

Dapper leapt to his feet, pulling out the little table already equipped with iced water and a plate piled high with slices of buttered brown bread.

'You look wonderful,' he said, and glanced at the waitress who was primed to produce two tankards of pink champagne.

'Mmm,' said Laura. 'This is rather a treat.'

He nodded, admiring her serpentine figure and wide full lips. The satisfaction was mutual because his broad shoulders and slightly crooked smile did him no harm in her eyes.

'Will you marry me?' He had leant forwards and taken her free hand in his, turning it and kissing the palm just before he spoke.

If Laura was surprised, she concealed it well. She gave his hand an answering squeeze, and took another sip from the tankard.

'That's what I like about you, Dapper,' she said, smiling. 'No messing around.'

'You know,' he said, giving her the full benefit of his yellow wide-eyed stare, 'that I love you very much.'

'Thank you,' she said, agreeably aware that conversation was suddenly somewhat out of fashion at the neighbouring tables.

'Would you both like to . . .' the waitress had returned but her habitual sentence died away in the face of Dapper's cold glare.

'Oh yes!' said Laura. 'I'm ravenous. Let's order.'

'OK,' Dapper glanced at the menu. 'I'll have lobster cocktail and a Dover sole, grilled on the bone, with some mashed swede. What about you?'

'That sounds perfect,' said Laura cosily. 'I'll have the same.'

'Well?'

Laura sat and thought. He was very attractive. He made her laugh. She could well afford to marry whom she chose, even a profligate gambler like Dapper. She was not for one moment afraid of losing control of her financial stability. On the other hand, he was more than usually selfish, he would of course be habitually unfaithful, he might even be violent when drunk. None of that would overwhelm her if she loved him, but since she didn't, it was not a hard decision. What was hard, given that she had a kind heart and a natural sympathy for rogues, was to maintain some pretence of taking him seriously.

'It's a very great compliment,' she said at last.

'Meaning no!' he said, his smile dying away.

'The greatest compliment I have ever been paid.'

'Is there no hope?'

'My first proposal!'

'Could you not love me a little?'

'And deliciously public.'

'Look!' said Dapper, turning to the goggle-eyed couple at the adjacent table. 'Haven't you some other subject to occupy your attention during lunch?'

'Sorry, old boy,' murmured the man, a school contemporary of Dapper's. He and his companion closed in on each other and started whispering.

'Not a smidgeon of affection?' He turned back to Laura with an air of self-mockery.

'Oh yes,' she said. 'I adore you. You're my very best friend in the world. Your eyes are unforgettable. But I could never marry you. It would be like incest.'

'My grandfather was very keen on incest.'

'I dare say,' said Laura drily. 'Ooh look! There's Daddy coming in with Perky.' She waved madly, to receive an embarrassed nod from her father who had just begun to retreat at the sight of his daughter's profile.

'You know Dapper, Daddy, don't you?' Max kissed his daughter perfunctorily and shook hands frostily with her companion.

'How *are* you, Perky?' continued the irrepressible Laura, kissing her on both cheeks. 'Mmm! You smell absolutely delicious. I just love Eau de Paradis.'

Perky laughed and Max took her arm.

'Do you know Dapper?' Laura said. 'Perky Metternich, Dapper Gumby.'

Perky acknowledged the yellow stare. 'We don't want to interrupt you,' she said. 'Your father and I are just having a snack before driving down to Glyndebourne.'

'Ooh, are those real?' Laura's eyes had zeroed in on a heavy bracelet of chunky red stones wound round the other woman's black gloved wrist.

'Now Laura, do get on with your lunch,' said Max impatiently, 'and leave Perky's rubies alone.' He almost hauled her away, leaving his daughter staring after them.

'Gosh,' she said. 'Emeralds last month. Now rubies. What does that woman *do* to him?'

The couple at the next table leant forward as one, and then cringed back as Dapper made as if to turn on them again.

'Mr Gumby?' This time it was a waiter. 'Telephone call.'

'God almighty!' groaned Dapper. 'We'd have had more peace in the middle of Hyde Park Corner.' He walked over to where the man was holding out a receiver. 'Yes!' He listened for a bit. 'Yes. Fine. I understand. Half an hour. Goodbye.'

'Who was that?' Laura asked when he came back.
'My solicitor.'

'Goodness, how grand. Do you keep in touch with him on an hourly basis?'

He laughed. 'Not always. I'm being pursued at the moment. You probably read about the Sarti débacle?'

'Well of course I remember when he shot himself. Daddy was upstairs in the Clermont at the time.'

Dapper nodded. 'He made a fool of me. But since he's dead, that's water under the bridge. What were we saying?'

'Well,' said Laura. 'You were saying that your grandfather enjoyed incest.'

'And you were saying that you wouldn't marry me.'

'*What* an interesting conversation,' observed Perky as she walked past on her way to the cloakroom. 'You must tell me how it all turns out.'

They, like the rest of the room, watched her spectacular progress between the tables, smiling in recognition here, discreetly feigning oblivion there.

'Quite a character,' observed Laura, wryly acknowledging the admiration in Dapper's eyes.

'Yes,' he said distantly, since he was already worrying about how to pay the bill.

Half an hour later, Dapper walked up the steps of White's, waved a friendly greeting to Stinson, the duty porter, and strode through to the bar where he found Tim discussing the latest opinion polls with Jim Lubbock, the new Environment Minister. Detaching his solicitor, the two of them moved through to a small banquette behind the billiards table.

'So what's the fuss?'

Tim explained.

'You mean I could be hauled up in court?'

'Yes. Why on earth did you sign that paper without consulting me?'

'Well, there wasn't any particular significance about it, was there? Bob Mackay said it was just a belt-and-braces procedure to avoid another expensive set of correspondence.'

'All it did was commit you to apply everything you had to paying off your debts to them. It also specified the proceeds of the contents of Gumby.'

'Yes, well he'd been asking about that.'

'So what's with the Mount Street Casino?'

Dapper whistled. 'There's no privacy in this world.'

'Go on.'

'Well, of course, I owed them a lot of money. They'd been advancing me quite a bit.'

'That's illegal for a start.'

'Really? Anyway, I had a plunge to try to retrieve the situation.'

'And lost the lot?'

'Almost. I had enough left in cash to pay off the bookmakers and a couple of other old friends.'

'Not your solicitors by any chance?' Tim grinned.

'No,' said Dapper, and took the other man by the arm. 'You've been a good friend through all this. I hope it won't get you into trouble with those two sharks you work with.'

'So how was lunch?' Tim had been bursting to ask.

'Fun but no dice.'

'She won't marry you?'

'Nope, but at least she paid the bill.'

'Well.' They looked at each other. 'Relatives? God-parents?'

'No-one. Or, at least, no-one who can help. It must be over a million not counting the tax you talked about at the time.'

'Nothing left?' It was scarcely believable.

'Nothing, apart from the picture sale at Garrisons next week.'

They stared at the floor in silence.

At last Tim stood up. 'I don't hold out much hope, but I'll see what I can do with my senior partner. There must be some way of buying you some breathing space.'

'Thanks,' said Dapper and Tim left him there, leafing through an old copy of *Country Life*.

Chapter 10

After parting from Dapper on the corner of St James's Street, Laura walked down the hill, fed some more money into her parking meter, and turned east into Pall Mall. She belonged to a club of her own, a modest ménage, just a luncheon room with a couple of small but beautifully decorated reading rooms on the first floor of an apartment block. There was no-one in whom she knew, a couple of old ladies up from the country and an American in a jazzy shirt, so she settled down in an armchair by the window to think.

She was not entirely happy with the course her life was taking. She had enjoyed school, a great grey greasy castle in the Home Counties set about with playing fields. It had been a welcome relief from home, where her parents had conducted room to room guerrilla warfare with scant regard for the only innocent bystander. The *casus belli* varied, but the roar of parental artillery rarely abated. First it had been about money, then her father's drinking, and finally Maria, who had been his mistress for nearly ten years. Nately Towers had seemed an oasis of security by contrast, with its winding staircases, avenues of yew, and laurel thickets where a courageous cigarette could be passed round in companionable guilt. One or two local boys had endeavoured to undress her with varying degrees of finesse, one even taking the daring step of showing her his inflated quivering member, an unappetizing pole of gristle that made her nearly sick with laughter.

A year in Florence, improving her Italian and deciding her forever to forego the messy pleasures of painting in oils, had been followed by a dismal round of silent cocktail parties, and, worse, the false camaraderie of the charity balls. She was bored by race courses, disliked the indiscriminate slaughter of small birds, and loathed the gangling young men who told her dirty stories by way of witty conversation. And yet, through all this, she knew herself to be companionable, to be capable of enjoying life and, above all, to be eager to love and be loved. It was not that she was spoilt, she told herself grimly, it was just that she had not as yet found a niche among the empty pleasures her preoccupied parents had chosen for her.

Curiously enough, it was her money that had set her free. Her first visit to Ruggles, Cavendish and Bryce had come as a great shock. She had known, of course, that her parents were not really short of money. There was a big house, land, servants, expensive motor cars, the usual comfortable circumstances of the affluent, the trivia that somehow seem so much more enticing to those who lack them than to those for whom they are an unconsidered backdrop, serving only to promote other circumstances into the field of drama: her mother's nerves, for example, or the strange stain in the pantry.

'Mr Ruggles wants to meet you properly,' her father had said, driving her up to London in the big black and silver car that smelled of dead meat. 'You'll be twenty-one next month and thank God I shan't have to pay you your allowance after that.'

'Oh good,' she had said. 'Does that mean I can go out and look for a job?'

He had glared at her sourly. 'You can do what you choose,' he had said, 'since your grandfather apparently placed more confidence in your generation than in mine.'

The facts and figures had swum in front of her. The next day she had driven herself into the local market town and bought every book she could find on finance. The day after her birthday, she had taken the train to London, walked round Knightsbridge until she had found a convenient flat, and persuaded Mr Ruggles to pay the asking price forthwith. Now, two years later, she felt qualified to manage her own affairs as and when it would be necessary for her to do so. That would be a job in its own right.

Meanwhile, it was time for her to find something absorbing and useful to do. Not least because of her secret. It was a big secret, and sometimes she had felt a violent need to talk about it. But who to? She was, of course, in love. But the man she loved seemed as remote from her as could be, and she could see no immediate way of lessening the distance, since it was largely her own fault.

When she had first met Tim, she had seen him almost as a family servant. Indeed, her parents always talked scathingly about the lawyers who regulated their affairs, referring to them with the same contempt they extended to their own staff. She had been old enough to feel distaste for this attitude, but not quite old enough to have shaken off all the symptoms of its baleful inoculation. She had been half way towards acknowledging him to herself as an extremely attractive if older man rather than the colourless automaton her father ignored, when

Tim, looming over her, had suddenly and quite unexpectedly asked her to go out with him and some unspecified friends. Her instinctive unthinking response had been as accidental as it had been insulting. She read her own shame in his confused, then mortified, expression, and perhaps it was the care he took to smooth over the ensuing silence that made her begin to appreciate his character, as well as his appearance. But since that evening five years ago, he had barely acknowledged her existence, except in their professional dealings when he treated her with impeccable if distant politeness.

She indulged herself for ten minutes now, reflecting on his beauty, and on his rare but rewarding smile. But she saw, and puzzled over, a wariness in his eyes, a vulnerability, that was at strange odds with his jutting chin. She had never dared ask her father about him, lest he guess her secret. She knew he would only mock her affections.

'More tea, Miss?' The comfortable middle-aged waitress had waddled up, an early candidate for a hip replacement, Laura guessed.

'No thank you, Winnie,' she said. 'I must be moving on.'

'More shopping?' asked the waitress with a smile that came more from the head than from the heart. Perhaps she would have judged Laura less harshly if she had known how gladly she would have exchanged places.

'No fear!' laughed Laura. 'I'm off to improve my mind in the National Gallery.'

'It's all right for some,' muttered Winnie to herself, gathering up the little tea set painted with violets and carrying it off painfully to the kitchen. Two hours to go before she could catch the bus home to Kilburn where her sister would be sleeping off her morning's investment in the wine trade. A bell rang above her head.

'Oh I'm coming,' she grumbled aloud. 'It's that dratted American cow again.' Fixing a smile precariously in place, she began her slow way back to the world of chintz and porcelain.

Out in the street again, Laura walked along to the traffic lights and, on an impulse, turned north up the Haymarket. What form was her contribution to the world to take? Certainly her mother's example had inoculated her for ever against playing at toy charities. She knew, for example, that the theatre she was walking past had been booked en bloc the following night for a gala performance in aid of Cupboard Love, a small but socially exclusive charity organized by Lady Woodchester under Royal patronage.

No doubt it was unfair of her to mock these and similar efforts of her mother's circle to raise money for controversial, even grubby, causes by shrouding them in the comfortable disguise of social events. But she felt that her own efforts, even if not impelled by the usual pressure to earn more money, would be more enthusiastic if geared to real personal achievement. But what? Her qualifications – a reasonable aptitude for figures plus fluency in French and Italian – would probably get her a job in an art gallery; and her looks, of which she was realistically aware, would be no handicap in an auction house or a fashion magazine. But none of this had any appeal.

Finding that she had now reached Piccadilly Circus, she crossed the busy road and was wandering aimlessly towards Leicester Square, when suddenly she recognized Tim, on his way back from White's, hurrying past her. She made to call out to him, but checked herself, unwilling to precipitate a conversation with him without some preparation. So she stood still and watched, wistfully following his head growing smaller until it was lost in the crowd.

If I am to seem worthwhile to him, she thought, I must soon find myself something to do.

Chapter 11

It was six o'clock to the minute that same evening when Laura opened her door to Robin Ruggles and saw with a sinking heart that he was carrying a vast sheaf of livid orange roses.

'Goodness me!' she said. 'What on earth have you got there?'

'For you!' he said, thrusting the garish bundle at her.

'Mmm,' she said, sniffing them in vain since they had come straight from refrigeration. This restricted their immediate effect to the release of a stream of cold water drops down her silk dress.

'I thought you'd like them,' he said with a smirk.

Well, you thought wrong, her mind silently contradicted him, as she smiled her way towards an empty vase.

'Can we sit for a moment?'

'Oh,' she said, 'isn't the private view at six-thirty?'

'Yes,' he replied, taking an unwilling hand in his, 'but it goes on till eight.'

'Well, come and have a quick drink then. But I have to be back before eight, because I have an old aunt coming for dinner.'

Robin's face fell, but he rallied as her sofa came into view.

'I've just got some white wine, or would you like something stronger?'

'White wine would be perfect.'

She poured out two glasses and sat firmly on an armchair, ignoring his companionable gesture inviting her to join him.

'Laura.'

Oh no, she thought. Oh *no*! But there he was, well and truly on one knee. Couldn't one accept any invitation without it opening the door to sex or marriage? Had she really laid herself open to a second proposal in one day?

'Darling!' he said, sprawling towards her. 'I love you madly. Please say you will do me the honour of becoming my wife.'

'No,' she said. 'No.'

'No?'

'No.'

'Nothing more?'

'Nothing more.' She stood up, suddenly angry. Yes, she'd accepted occasional evenings out to see a film or play tennis. No. She had never let him kiss her. Not, in fact, she immediately recalled, that he had ever tried. And now this!

'Well, I must say.'

'What?'

'Well – you might take some time to consider it.'

She turned away, made a strong effort, and turned back with a good-natured grin.

'Robin. Get up. Let's go to this private view while we're about it. How can you propose to a girl when you've never even found out if she wanted to kiss you.'

'Oh *well*,' he said, bounding to his feet. 'If that's all,' and lumbered towards her.

'No!' she shrieked. 'No!' as she found herself encircled, almost enveloped, by a massive amalgam of damp flesh and rotting tweed. 'You smell awful!'

He trod backwards, upsetting a small table, spilling its collection of glass animals to destruction on the parquet floor.

'There's someone else!' he said. 'That's it, isn't it?'

She was on the floor, trying to salvage the glass octopus her father had given her to start the little collection.

'Isn't it?' He had grabbed her arm, was shaking her.

'Yes,' she said. 'Yes! Now let go of me and stop making such a scene.'

'Gumby, I suppose. That slick-haired layabout. Well, he's out of the running. He was arrested this evening.'

Laura stared at him. 'Arrested?' she said, shocked.

'Yes – arrested.' Robin's face was scarlet, with drops of sweat running down his forehead. 'And not a moment too soon. So you can forget *him*. Now what about me?' He was still holding her sleeve.

'I think you should leave,' she said as calmly as she could. 'I must start preparing dinner for my aunt.'

'Fuck you!' he shouted. 'Fuck you and fuck your money!'

It was only then that she realized he was very drunk. 'Off you go,' she said kindly. 'Shall I call a taxi?'

He lurched out of the room and she heard the outer door slam. Shortly afterwards there was a squeal of tyres and, twice, the sound of an angry horn.

She continued to pick up the broken glass animals. Then she went into the kitchen, grabbed the roses and threw them into the bin. She started to prepare dinner, chopping up some tomatoes for the soup, and smearing olive oil on to the two silvery mackerel that she had bought on her way home. Suddenly she started crying.

When her aunt arrived an hour later, she had recovered her poise and was in the final stages of liquidizing the soup.

'Aunt Gwen!' They kissed each other with real warmth.

'Laura my dear. You look very worn out.'

She smiled. 'I am rather.'

'One of those days?'

'I hope not. I couldn't manage too many like today.'

'Leave that and come and sit down,' said her aunt, a round, red-faced woman with long silver hair impeccably done up with a bun. She was smartly dressed in a dark blue suit over a speckled blouse with a high choker secured by a single large diamond.

Laura sat beside her obediently, having poured them both some wine.

'You look like someone who has had an unwelcome proposal.'

'Oh Aunt Gwen!' cried Laura. 'You are such a clairvoyant. Only I've had *two*!'

'Two in one day. You lucky thing! I rarely had two in one year!'

Laura pointed at the smashed animals, and her aunt raised her eyebrows.

'It must be that lovely dress,' she said. 'Pink suits you.'

'I never encouraged them, not once.'

'Well,' said her aunt. 'Of course things are rather different nowadays. In my time, you could go out with a man for a year without implying anything beyond friendship. These days I believe if you let him buy you a snack, he expects instant bunking.'

'Bonking.' Laura corrected her with a smile.

'Whatever. That's better. But it's true. I was talking to Maimie Woodchester about it at lunch. She says even a cup of coffee means they can expect a kiss. Though what she would know about it at her age, Heaven only knows.'

'All I did was go out to dinner with them a couple of times.' Well, Laura thought, perhaps three or four times.

'No hanky panky?'

'Of course not!'

'No necking?'

'Really, Aunt Gwen, where do you hear these expressions?'

The older woman laughed. 'I have every edition of *The Lady's Journal* since it started in the fifties. I read them through, and then I start again. That and the Law Reports.'

'The Law Reports?'

'Yes, my dear. I'm having trouble with my landlord, so I'm boning up on the Law of Property and Contract.'

'But I thought Scrymgeour Square was on the Chesterfield Estate.'

'So it is.'

'Well surely they . . .'

'Surely they nothing. A bunch of sharks, especially that mad old lecher. Did you read about him beating his poor girlfriend?'

Laura shook her head. 'No. When?'

'Oh, just the other day. He beat her unconscious and the police arrived only just in time to save her. That's my landlord for you! Now where's this dinner you promised me? We need to talk about your father. He is about to make rather a fool of himself, I'm afraid.'

Elsewhere in the city, the subject of this prediction lay sprawled across Perky in a state of comatose delight. His head was between her breasts and she was delicately massaging his spine.

'Thank you,' she whispered and drew up her long legs so that she could run one foot along the back of his thigh. 'That was lovely.'

He raised his head and looked into her eyes, half hooded now beneath their slanted brows. 'I love you,' he murmured.

She smiled and arched her neck to kiss his lips. 'Oh, don't leave me,' she moaned.

'It's quite involuntary,' he said. 'I love your smell.'

'Pass me those tissues.'

She watched him groan as he stretched over to the bedside table. I'm lucky, she thought. I really enjoy my work. Perhaps because it's entertainment. Actors, singers, players, harlots. People pay us to do what we enjoy. But it's lucky I like older men. Having decided it was too soon to start talking about diamonds, she found herself thinking about the man she'd seen proposing to Laura at lunch. He really was startlingly attractive, and not so much older than her. Forty at the most. But 'Dapper'! What a ridiculous name. She couldn't imagine bedding a man called 'Dapper'. Anyway. Max had said he was going bust. So that ruled him out.

'My poor friend!' she said aloud.

'No,' protested Max weakly. 'I'm very tired.' Perky rolled him over.

'Well,' she said, 'let me see what *I* can do.'

Chapter 12

'That's the view from the top of the Lecht.' Flora had brought her photograph album for Tim to see. 'That's my father.'

'The one in leggings?'

'Yes – he was loading for one of Major Fitzwilliam's guests.'

'And who's that?'

She laughed. 'That's me, with my pet duck.'

'It looks very fierce.'

'Yes,' she giggled. 'She was a bit of a tartar.'

'She?'

'Mmm. She was called Elspeth. She laid lots of eggs.'

Tim leant over to reach the teapot. 'I want to talk about you.'

'Not again.'

'You've got to leave the Colonel.'

'But where would I go?'

They had had this conversation so often that it creaked with unspoken innuendoes. He knew she wanted him to ask her to move in with him; she knew he wanted her to volunteer to abandon her only source of income.

'That's a different question, surely.'

'Not if you haven't got any money,' she retorted bitterly.

He ran his fingers through her thick pale hair,

uncertain of his own feelings towards her. Did he love her enough to face the whispers, even open scandal, that marriage to her might bring? They had passed Laura with some friends coming out of the same restaurant a couple of nights before. He was still smarting from the disdainful glint in her eyes before she had turned her back on Flora and hurried away into the night. Bloody little snob! But was it a bad sign that he should even be thinking such careful, pompous thoughts? He hadn't even begun to explore the problem of the Colonel, and his likely response to losing a beautiful young mistress to his legal adviser. And what on earth would the Ruggleses say?

It wasn't exactly that Tim thought the less of her for her unconventional lifestyle, but undoubtedly it acted as a focus for his own internal misgivings, the same misgivings that had plagued, and eventually destroyed, all his previous liaisons.

'Why do you keep bringing money into it?' he asked sourly, conscious as he spoke that his words were empty and offensive. She shrugged, gazing sadly into his eyes. On an impulse, she lifted one of his hands and kissed it.

Looking down into her golden curls, still matted and damp from their exertions upstairs, Tim half lifted his right arm to encircle her delicate shoulders and pull her to him, to accept her love, and thus responsibility for her future. What held him back? Was the bony outline of her shoulderblade through the thin cotton blouse too frail to appeal to someone himself in need of support? Or was there some subliminal resemblance to his mother that, recalling his early taste of feminine betrayal, kept him aloof? Even a glancing thought on this made him flinch. He dropped his arm and Flora, sensing something like hostility, slid away from him.

'Tim?' she whispered. 'What is it?'

He shook his head. What, after all, did he seek through marriage? Companionship? Children? Or the reassurance of love? What about giving? What could he give, when he was so obsessed with the potential for betrayal, apart from money? And in that case, would he not be buying love as directly as the Colonel? Again he bucked his head, but violently, and in mentally brushing aside this uncomfortable introspection, he physically swept his teacup on to the floor.

'What *is* the matter?' she said, staring at him in alarm.

The telephone added a further jangle to their confusion.

'Yes. Tim Bryce. Who?'

She watched him talking spasmodically, his tension eased by an automatic assumption of his professional manner, the calm, thoughtful family solicitor. This was perhaps their tenth evening alone, the Colonel being away in Staffordshire on official duties. And it had followed a familiar course – a cheerful telephone chat, a cosy dinner in a small bistro, with the atmosphere thickening as their thoughts turned towards bed. Then back to his house, an hour or so of physical concentration, and then The Subject. Somehow The Subject was always her. It was she who was implied to be in need of a change, she on whom the onus rested to do something.

Rebelliously, she was beginning to wonder if she could not turn the tables by suggesting that his own life might benefit from a little positive action. Less drinking, perhaps? More emotional commitment even? The void in his heart was as public as a scarlet birthmark. Not least, she presumed, because it was not naturally there. He was not vain, nor even especially selfish. He was invariably kind to her, thoughtful in entertaining her and, best of all, he made her laugh. But the frosted panel that obscured the view to his heart served more efficiently as a prison wall than as a protection. Just as others could not see in, so he presently could not see out. And Flora no longer believed that she had the key to free him. Her self-confidence was rooted in her body, not in her mind, which she felt to be at a disadvantage in learning, if not in quickness and understanding. And what man wants to be understood?

Involuntarily she smiled up at him where he stood listening to the telephone.

'Say nothing until I arrive,' he said. 'Do you understand?'

Evidently satisfied by the reply, he replaced the receiver and came over to her. 'I must run you home, I'm afraid.'

'Trouble?'

'Yes. One of my clients has been arrested. I must go and sort it out.'

'I'll just get a taxi.'

'Certainly not,' he said, 'it's on my way. What were you smiling about?'

'You,' she said, noting the flicker of alarm in his expression. 'You looked so earnest.'

'I am earnest,' he protested, also smiling. 'It's part of the job.'

'That's why I love you,' she said, and in the silence that followed, she resolved that the least painful way out was not to see him again.

It was nearly ten o'clock when Tim reached the Shepherd Street police station. Parking carefully on a single yellow line, he hurried in to find the duty sergeant arguing with a drunken man in evening dress.

'You have a client of mine here,' he interrupted. 'Mr Gumby.'

'Oh yes, sir,' replied the sergeant, only too pleased for a respite. 'He's in Interview Room Number Six. May I see your card? Now come along, Mr Rose,' he said, turning back to the little round man whose crinkled wig had slipped to one side, exposing a strangely discoloured scalp. 'Wouldn't it be better if you just went home. I'm sure the young lad meant no harm.'

'Poor old soul!' confided the sergeant as they walked down the dull green corridor. 'It's always the same. He thinks every young tearaway is interested in him. Pathetic really.'

Dapper leapt up when Tim entered the room. It was bare apart from an old metal desk and three plastic chairs, and he had been sitting there for nearly four hours.

'Thank God you've come,' he said, warmed by Tim's friendly supportive smile and general aura of confidence.

'Would you both like a cup of tea?' enquired the sergeant, whose own manner was subtly changed in favour of Dapper by the positive impression made by Tim.

'I wouldn't if I were you,' warned Dapper.

Tim smiled. 'Yes please,' he said. 'Now,' he went on, sitting down at the desk and taking a thick notebook from his briefcase, 'what exactly has happened?'

'I've been arrested!'

'For?'

'Fraud.'

'When?'

'When I got back this evening. Say half past five. There were two men in hideous suits waiting.'

'Why didn't you ring me immediately?'

'I did. I got through to that fat slug, Robin Ruggles. He said he would deal with it.'

'I never heard a word.'

'No. Nor did I! No-one came. I only remembered I had your home number an hour ago and they let me use the telephone again.'

'Have you been asked any questions?'

'Quite a few. But after they read out that caution, I thought I'd better wait till you came.'

'Absolutely right. Have they said anything about charging you?'

'Oh yes. I've been formally charged.'

'So why are you still here?'

'Because they only got round to that after I'd spoken to you.'

'Well, we can go now. I'll drive you home. There's nothing more to be done till the morning. Then I can start finding out what the exact complaint against you is, and we can decide how best to counter it.'

'I knew you'd help.'

'Well, of course,' said Tim, who was privately rather surprised by his friend's pallor. 'I'm quite convinced it's a silly misunderstanding which we can easily sort out. Don't let it get to you! Now let's collect a copy of the charge and then go back to White's for a reviving drink.'

Chapter 13

'You say you never got the message?' Henry Ruggles looked up from his desk at Tim who was standing angrily in front of him.

'That's right.'

The old man pressed a button. 'Oh, Kenneth.'

'Yes, Mr Ruggles,' replied a tinny subservient voice.

'Could you ask Mr Robin to come and see me?'

There was a pause from the intercom. 'Mr Robin hasn't come in this morning.'

'Hasn't come in?' Henry looked at his wristwatch. 'It's nearly nine o'clock.'

'Yes, Mr Ruggles.'

Henry flipped another switch and pressed a series of buttons. The sound of an amplified dialling tone filled the room, then a female voice said, 'Good morning. How may I help you?'

'Carlotta?'

'Oh, yes, Mr Ruggles.'

'Has Mr Robin left?'

'Oh yes, Mr Ruggles. He came down shortly after you'd left. He didn't eat any breakfast – just drove away.'

'I see. Thank you, Carlotta.'

He flicked the switch back, shutting off the sound. 'Well, well,' he said to Tim. 'No doubt he'll join us soon. What have you discovered about the arrest?'

'Perry's must have gone straight to the police after I'd left. I don't know what could have changed their mind.'

'Have they a case?'

Tim thought. 'Yes and no.'

'Please explain.'

'Well . . .' The telephone rang again. The old man picked it up impatiently.

'Yes?' He frowned, then shrugged. 'Very well, Kenneth. Show her in. Gwendolyn Ingram. You'd better stay for this.'

Laura's aunt marched into the room and shook them both by the hand.

'Sorry to be so early in the day,' she said, 'but I have things to do.'

Henry Ruggles bowed expressively. If he always used a little flattery with his clients, with the Ingrams he applied it in massive doses.

'How may we help?'

'Well,' she said, taking out a thin pair of spectacles and peering through them at an irregular piece of paper. 'I want you to issue an injunction against my landlord.'

Silence fell.

'Well?' she demanded querulously. 'Can you do it?'

Henry Ruggles cast a brief appealing look at Tim.

'The problem is,' said the latter gently, 'this firm is retained by your landlords. I'm presuming you're referring to your Chesterfield Square house.'

'I certainly am. I know it's being done on purpose. They've wrecked the gardens and now they're working every night in the house next door. It's been going on for months.'

'I'm very sorry to hear it,' put in Henry Ruggles.

If he had hoped for a softened response, he was mistaken.

'Do you mean to tell me,' demanded the old woman, 'that you, my own solicitor, won't act for me when I need you most?'

Henry Ruggles spread his hands. 'We're in a very awkward position,' he said.

'I'll say you are,' she retorted robustly. 'Does that mean you'll be on the other side?'

The two men stared at each other again.

'I'm sure not,' said Tim, catching the hesitation in his senior partner's eyes. 'But it is possible.'

'Well in that case, I'd better keep my powder dry, hadn't I?' she said, and marched out of the room just as the squat little clerk was bringing in a tray of coffee and toast.

'I suppose we're lucky this has never happened before,' said Tim as he opened the marmalade.

The other man grunted. 'I can see this is going to be a bad day,' he said. 'I can't say I wasn't warned.'

Tim raised his eyebrows.

'My horoscope,' Henry Ruggles explained. 'It's always right. This morning it said "The influence of Saturn, the Black Sun, combined with revolutionary Uranus in your mid-heaven, will exert unusual pressure on aspects of your working life". As soon as I opened the newspaper, I just knew there'd be trouble.' With a deep sigh, he gulped down some coffee.

'Where *is* Robin?'

It was two hours later and they had agreed, thanks to Tim's persuasive support, to continue to represent Dapper. As for a Chesterfield-Ingram dispute, they would certainly have to act for the Colonel, since it was an integral part of their work for his company. As Laura's Aunt Gwen was one of the older generation, explicitly placed in the Trustees' hands with no release save death, the firm had little to lose from her displeasure. Indeed, since the allocation of her income was decided by Henry Ruggles (ostensibly acting with the elusive General Morne), it was scarcely in her interests to risk offending her provider. Thus had her father's Will promoted their family's employee into their master.

But it was a measure of Henry Ruggles's shrewdness that he had never succumbed to the temptation to exercise this power visibly. He never wavered from his courteous, even obsequious, treatment of the five older life tenants committed to his care, and, what was even more of a triumph, he had successfully taught his son to adopt the same subservience. Any adverse decisions were laid at the door of the distant General, a man who thus in his absence had acquired a formidable place in the family demonology.

Tim got up. 'I'll have to go now. Let me know when Robin comes in. We need to sort out what went wrong with the system last night.'

The old man didn't look up. He knew as well as Tim that his son had defied every convention by abandoning their client.

As Tim walked back down the corridor, one of the junior solicitors put her head round the door and called his name.

'Hello Judy,' he said. 'What can I do for you?'

'Could you come in here for a second?'

He walked into her office.

She looked nervous, and gestured to him to sit down. 'I don't quite know how to say this,' she said.

He smiled encouragingly. Boy friend trouble? A difficult client?

'Mr Robin didn't come in this morning,' she said.

'I know.'

'We had a call from Kleinworts about the Clients' Account overnight money.'

'So?'

She paused, and bit anxiously at a fingernail. He waited.

'I had to check on Mr Robin's computer.'

'And?'

'The figures don't tally.'

He understood now why she was so pale. 'Are you sure?'

'Oh yes.' She laughed, a high-pitched noise that held little amusement. 'I've checked it over and over again.'

'How much is missing?'

'Twelve and a half thousand pounds.'

'Out of?'

'A hundred and sixty-eight thousand.'

'I see.'

'Was I right to tell you?'

He looked at her. Pale, anorexic, she had the intense air of a mature student. He knew her to be hardworking, slightly humourless, and an expert on conveyancing. This was her first good job, and she had held it for four years. But what future was there for a junior employee who caught the son of the house pilfering from his father?

'Yes,' he said. 'Of course you were. We'll say

nothing to Mr Ruggles until I've had a chance to talk to Robin.' He smiled what he hoped was a reassuring smile and left. Whoever wrote the Senior Partner's horoscope clearly had a keen eye for planetary influence in High Holborn.

Chapter 14

The reason for Robin's absence was simple. Having now no need for the engagement ring he had borrowed from the office to buy, he had naturally decided to take it back and retrieve the money. Since he was a new customer, the shop had refused a credit card, and having left his cheque book at home, withdrawing the cash from the Clients' Account had seemed the simplest expedient. Partners often needed to make large cash withdrawals, and it had just been a case of looking the office cashier straight in the face and asking for it.

What he hadn't bargained for was that the shop, off Regent Street, didn't open that morning until after eleven. What was worse, when he arrived he found Max Ingram and a tall young woman in a scarlet scarf also waiting outside. He had tried to turn away but Max recognized him.

'Hello Ruggles!' he shouted 'Investing the clients' cash in diamonds, are you?'

Robin's face was a battlefield bloodily fought over by mingled guilt, astonishment and dismay.

'Do you know Miss Metternich?' persisted Max, who was clearly in a euphoric mood. 'My solicitor. Mr – er – Ruggles.'

Robin took her hand. It was cool and slender. He gazed at her, drinking in the charm of her allure. She looked away, embarrassed by his goat-like stare, and surreptitiously wiped away the dampness left by his touch. For half an hour they stood there, making desultory conversation, until at last the couple who owned the shop came laughing up the street.

'Hello, Major Ingram,' said the woman, smiling broadly as anyone would to such a lavish client. Her husband, who had served Robin the previous afternoon, gave him a more cautious greeting. He had half expected to find him there – jewellers being not unaccustomed to men returning engagement rings.

'That's no problem,' he whispered discreetly, understanding that Robin knowing his other customers would redouble his desire for privacy. They waited till Max and Perky had gone to the opposite counter. Then Robin handed back the little velvet-lined box, and the jeweller returned the thick brown envelope of fifty pound notes he had locked in the safe overnight. Cash customers were quite usual. He'd known necklaces paid for with suitcases of currency. After Robin had hurried out, the jeweller went over to join Max and Perky.

'Yes indeed!' he said, as his wife held up the heavy diamond drop earrings against Perky's face. 'Those look lovely on you. They're Cartier, of course. Made for Lady Castlemaine in nineteen twenty-three, I think. Flawless.'

Max gazed at Perky's face reflected in the little mirror on the showcase. Her brown eyes were glowing like the pendants. His gaze dropped, piercing her clothes, recollecting her body. As he stood there, in a daze of desire, the two jewellers watched him covertly. In three months he had spent over eighty thousand pounds in their shop; if this went on, they would be able to buy the Greek villa that they had so often fantasized about. So many dreams were built on this woman's supple frame.

'Will you send me the bill?'

'Of course.' The jeweller bowed. 'May I wrap them for you?'

While his wife was fussing about with tissue paper, Perky took her lover's hand. 'Thank you,' she said. 'They're wonderful.'

He smiled down at her. What more could life offer?

Chapter 15

That weekend, Laura drove down to Dorset. Her mother had telephoned twice during the week, sounding more querulous each time.

'I never see you, darling,' she had said, 'nor your father for that matter. Though perhaps that's a mercy.'

'Oh come on. He's not that bad!' Laura had protested, half-heartedly, and in the end, reluctantly, she had pretended that she had always intended to be going back for a couple of days.

Milston was a small village scattered about a deep valley where two streams met to become almost a river. The manor house, a long rectangular house of golden stone, had been built in the seventeenth century by a man with a taste for elaborate windows. Whatever frustrations he may have felt in the rest of his endeavours, he had allowed none in his imaginative use of decoration for his house. Deep carved oriels stretched from earth to attic, every façade was encrusted with pilasters, and even the smallest dormer had its own stone pediment. Gargoyles squinted out from beneath the eaves, and a positive forest of curlicued chimneys jutted out behind the alternate lions and griffons that guarded the jumbled roof, baring their teeth in a show of petrified menace.

But those who entered expecting further frenzy

within were disappointed. Whether the money had run out, as Max maintained, or whether some terrible fire had destroyed the interior, as an architectural historian had nervously suggested, inside there was simply a disappointing succession of plain rooms, innocent both of panelling and even of cornicing. Laura's mother had employed a firm of Sloane Street decorators to install their house style, and thus Milston had become a piece of Dorset which was forever Mayfair.

As Laura swung her car through the lodge gates, she caught sight of an old man standing in the doorway. He raised his hand and she stopped.

'Why, Bob! How are you?'

The old man beamed, and made his way painfully to his garden gate. 'I'm very well, Miss Laura, as you can see.'

'You look wonderful,' she said, taking in his troubled breathing and the angry scarlet of his cheeks. 'And Maisie?'

He shook his head. 'It's her day at the clinic,' he said. 'They take her every Friday, you know. She'd be so pleased to hear you were asking after her. But,' he leant closer, 'she's not as well as she was. The Major wants her to see someone in London, but she won't go. Won't even hear of it. She's that stubborn!'

Laura laughed. 'She certainly knows her mind,' she said. 'It's so nice to see you.'

The old man watched her drive off, and then slowly took out his pipe, the better to enjoy the sunshine.

'Old Bob doesn't look at all well,' Laura said to her mother as soon as she had joined her on the terrace.

'Are you sure you won't have some tea, darling?'

'No thanks. And what's wrong with Maisie?'

'Oh darling, I don't know. She must be eighty. Why your father keeps them in the lodge, I can't imagine. They ought to be in a home.'

'But Mother! They've always lived there. They'd hate to be shut up.'

Amanda Ingram shook her head as she untangled a thread in the tapestry cover she was working on. 'We ought to have someone younger in the lodge, for security.'

Laura stared at her mother, then looked away.

'So how was London?'

'Very hot. Is Father coming down?'

'Oh darling! How would I know? I'd be the very last person he'd tell. Yes, Stubbs? What is it now?'

A short man with a brown face, looking very hot in a tight black jacket, had hurried out of the French windows.

'It's the Major, madam. He's on the telephone.'

'Oh do I have to?' She rose grudgingly and flung down the tapestry. 'What now, I wonder?' Her footsteps echoed as she crossed the flagstones. The little man winked at Laura who laughed.

'Nice to have you here, Miss Laura.'

'You know perfectly well I loathe being called *Miss* Laura, Stubbs. What happened to your Lally?'

'She grew up,' he replied gravely. 'Into a very beautiful young woman.'

Unexpectedly, she felt herself blushing. 'What would Mrs Stubbs say?' she said by way of diversion.

'I'd say he was a wicked flirt!' shouted a voice from a window above them. 'Welcome back, dear.' They both looked up to see a cheerful red face leaning out between two scowling gargoyles. 'Your mother needs a bit of company.'

Somewhere in the house a door slammed.

'Oh-oh,' said Stubbs. 'Here comes trouble,' and he hurried away as Amanda rushed back on to the terrace.

'It's too bad,' she said. 'Your father never thinks of anyone except himself. That was him on the telephone,' she said unnecessarily. 'He's coming down in time for dinner, and bringing your Aunt Gwendolyn. What's more, he's invited the Woodchesters for dinner tomorrow night. It's too bad of him.'

'But you like Aunt Gwen,' protested Laura. 'And the Woodchesters are your friends.'

'The trouble with your mother,' said Mrs Stubbs, as Laura sat beside her after tea while she ironed some napkins, 'is that she hasn't got enough to do.'

'What about the Red Cross?'

Mrs Stubbs sniffed. 'That's all very well in its own way,' she said, 'but what does it amount to? A couple of coffee mornings each month, dictating a few letters to Mrs Gascoigne in the Estate Office, and that dratted Christmas bazaar. She ought to keep herself busy, like you do.'

Laura made a face. 'But I don't, Mrs Stubbs. I don't feel I'm contributing anything at all.'

'It'll come.' The old woman chuckled. 'You'll see. It's early days for you. But your Ma is going downhill. She'll be on the bottle if the Major doesn't look out.'

'Now tell me about Bob and Maisie,' said Laura, unconsciously veering away from her own fears about her mother's predicament.

'Well,' said Mrs Stubbs, briskly folding the last napkin before taking on the pillowcases, 'they're neither as young as they used to be.'

'But Bob looked really feverish. And his breathing sounded off.'

'He always was a bit of a grampus, was Bob.' Mrs Stubbs smiled. 'When Stubbs was with the Major in Burma, Bob had to do all the man's work in your Granny's house. And goodness did he wheeze! "Bob Crawley," I used to say, "a few less Capstans and you might live a little longer." But look at him now, eighty-three and still enjoying life.'

'And Maisie?'

Mrs Stubbs pursed her lips. 'Well now,' she said, pausing for a moment and putting down the iron. 'She isn't what I'd call exactly well. Not that she's said anything, mind.'

Laura nodded energetically, anxious not to abort the signalled confidence.

'I *think* she may have waterworks trouble,' said Mrs Stubbs with a little grimace as though to apologize for the subject. 'Something to do with that bag they fitted her with.'

'Oh dear,' said Laura.

Somewhere in the house, a bell rang insistently.

'That'll be your father, dear. Now run along, or I'll be late getting the potatoes in.'

As Laura reached the door to the hall, she could already hear the angry metallic tone her father reserved exclusively for his wife.

Dinner the following night was not a success. Max and Lord Woodchester disappeared into the billiard room with a decanter of port immediately it was over, and her mother, who had been drinking heavily all evening, fell asleep on the sofa, leaving Laura to entertain her aunt and Lady Woodchester.

'How's the lawsuit?' she enquired.

'Bloody old goat!' scoffed her aunt. 'We'll teach him that respectable old ladies can't be dealt with in the same way as his bimbettes.'

'What do you mean?' Lady Woodchester, who had herself been quietly nodding off, woke up with a start. Her little pink eyes, ringed with a startling blue liner, glinted with malicious interest.

'Charles Chesterfield. Trying to get me and poor Teresa Lubbock out of our houses. The impudence of it!' Her voice sank to a whisper. 'She's got no legs, you know.'

'None at all?'

'Do you know, I think' said Laura's mother, who had also woken up as they were speaking, 'that men are becoming absolutely *unspeakable*!'

'Mother,' said Laura patiently, 'what . . .'

'Your father is the worst of the lot,' interrupted her mother. 'The whole world knows how he treats me. He's your brother, Gwen. Can't you do something about this Perky creature? Built like Battersea power station, I hear; very bulky and with her legs always stuck in the air.'

'Come on, my dear,' said Lady Woodchester, rising awkwardly to her feet, and stretching out an arm towards her hostess. 'I need to go upstairs. Will you show me the way?'

'Don't you know it by now?' said Amanda rather ungraciously. Her legs felt heavy, and she was quite comfortable where she was.

'Certainly not!' replied the other, misunderstanding. 'Although,' she added in an undertone to Laura, 'I'm probably the only woman round here who doesn't.' The two women, one lame, the other half drunk, wobbled unsteadily out of the room.

'You'd never credit it now,' confided Aunt Gwen

blearily, when she and Laura were finally alone, 'but I once had a bit of a knees-up with Charles Chesterfield myself.'

'You went dancing together?' There was a thunderous crash outside from the staircase, followed by the sound of Lady Woodchester cursing freely.

'My dear!' wheezed her aunt. One strand of hair, which had escaped from her bun, straggled across her cheek, giving her an unexpectedly louche air. 'I don't know about you young people, but when I have my knees in the air, the last thing on my mind is dancing.' Laura stared at her. 'I'll tell you about it. We were all in a house party at Croxteth just after the war with Hugh and Foxy. God but was it *dull*! Anyway, there I was in the library all alone with that wicked Charles. He was considered quite a catch in those days, he'd been frightfully brave in Crete, and he'd just inherited from his uncle, you know the sort of thing. I don't know why, but I was thinking away to myself how he absolutely reeked of *it*, when I noticed this hole.'

'What hole?' Despite her embarrassment, Laura was intrigued.

'The hole in his shoe. So I said, "You've got a hole in your shoe." And he said, "*You've* got a hole between your legs." You can imagine! I was absolutely speechless.'

'What happened then?' Laura was leaning forward, her face rapt.

'Then he said, "Is it draughty?" in the coolest of drawls. Because you see, he knew, the rascal. He absolutely knew what I was thinking. I *had* to have him after that. We scampered down the corridor and found a housemaid's cupboard under some service stairs. The earth may not have moved, but everything else did. You've never heard such a clattering of dustpans and mops . . .'

'Aunt Gwen!'

'I know! I don't know why I'm talking like this. I've drunk *far* too much, trying to keep your poor mother company.'

'What a drama!'

'Yes,' said Aunt Gwen. 'It may not rank high among the Great Love Stories of the World, but I can assure you, it made a deep impression on me.'

'Here you are!' The two men came into the room, laughing companionably. 'Hello! Where are the others?'

'Upstairs, or trying to get there,' replied Aunt Gwen equably. 'It's very good of you to join us.'

After the Woodchesters had finally gone home, and the household had retired to bed, there was a cautious knock on Laura's door. It was Aunt Gwen, looking very shamefaced.

'My dear,' she said, sitting gingerly on her niece's bed, 'please forgive me for such an awful drunken outburst. You must be so ashamed of your old aunt.'

Laura took her hand. 'Of course not,' she said with a smile. 'It was fascinating.'

'Promise you'll never breathe a word to anyone?'

'I promise.'

'Thank you, my dear. Now there's something else I want to talk to you about. You've met this Metternich woman?'

'Yes. I rather like her.'

'Do you indeed? Well, I don't know her, but a friend of mine who must be nameless was made nearly penniless by his infatuation with her. So I think you may have to be prepared to help wean your father from her in the not too distant future.' Aunt Gwen nodded her head several times to emphasize her point. 'Maybe take him abroad. He used to love Siena when we were children.'

'That might suit me too,' murmured Laura reflectively.

'Uh-oh!' said her aunt. 'Another broken heart in the family?'

Laura nodded, her mind full of the pretty little blonde she had seen with Tim. She had tried to smile at him, but he had just glared back, while fussing over the other girl's coat. 'I'll get over it,' she said robustly, 'but a trip abroad with Dad might help.'

'Anybody I know?' Aunt Gwen's eyes sparkled with eager complicity.

Laura shook her head. It was her secret and she intended that it should remain so. They chatted for a little longer and then, with a wide yawn, Aunt Gwen hauled herself up and shuffled away towards her own bedroom, closing Laura's door with great stealth.

It was a mark of Laura's innate generosity that she neither judged nor condemned Perky, not even in the casual malice of social gossip where the warmest of hearts may occasionally succumb to the lure of the easy gibe. She observed Perky's effect on her father, she envied her her sexual allure, and she was impressed by her relaxed sophistication.

'A common tart,' wheezed Lady Woodchester into the ear of the Minister a week later as she peered down at the expectant faces in the stalls from the reassuring eminence of the Royal Box.

'Who? Where?' said the Minister, his drowsiness dispelled.

'There!' Her portentous finger was aimed at Row B along which Perky was sinuously passing, presenting her perfectly rounded bottom to an inscrutable line of overseas clients of Perry's Bank. The Minister licked his lips, and shook his head with sad disapproval. If he remembered Lady Woodchester's constant boast that it had only taken one look at the Woodchester Business Machine Company balance sheet to convince her to ensnare its owner, he tactfully kept his reminiscences to himself.

There are more ways than one to barter sex for money, and in that, at least, Perky had more colleagues in society than they themselves would readily acknowledge. And whose men got the better bargain? In Perky's case (and Flora's) the contract was short, clear and easily disengaged. In that of Lady Woodchester, and so very many others, the sums were larger, the contracts longer, and the cost of disengagement colossal. Perhaps that is what qualifies as respectability? Nor is this sexual barter a one-way system. For every heiress, there are a hundred men who dream of spending her income, and of those perhaps a dozen who make the attempt.

For all Laura's beauty, it had been her money that had drawn both Dapper and Robin Ruggles into pursuit. No doubt the beauty made the pursuit more agreeable, but a monumental plainness would not have deterred them. People say that no-one works harder for their money than those who marry for it, but perhaps they say it more in pious hope than from personal experience.

Chapter 16

VENICE COMES TO HAMPSHIRE!
An architect's dream to build a city of Baroque palaces for wealthy commuters has been approved by local planners after an appeal that went all the way to the Rt Hon Jim Lubbock, the recently promoted Environment Minister.

The new development, covering eight hundred acres of land previously used for gravel extraction, will feature four miles of intersecting canals and nearly a hundred new homes.

'It's the most important project since Pericles rebuilt Athens,' enthused society architect Gervase Yeatley-Smith, the wunderkind of the burgeoning Pre-Palladian school of design, who recently completed Prince Arthur's spectacular new house on the Thames at Richmond.

But as bulldozers moved on to the site yesterday afternoon, Captain Legge, Chairman of the local Save our Village protest group, likened the scheme to the Tower of Babel.

'This is just a group of cynical developers making a fast buck under cover of architectural snobbery. This area needs more commuters like Belfast needs more bombs. They may have won this battle,' he told me darkly, 'but the war continues.'

* * *

For the fourth time Henry Ruggles pulled his heavy old car into a lay-by to re-read the paragraph that gave him such pleasure. He shook his head. This was intoxicating stuff. He had turned off the motorway north of Farnham and was now threading his way through narrow lanes until suddenly the hedges fell back and there he was in the middle of a forest of cranes and excavating machinery. It looked more like a busy harbour than the lush meadowland it had been before the discovery of gravel had enriched the local farmer and disturbed six centuries of peaceful grazing. Gervase Yeatley-Smith, resplendent in a scarlet helmet emblazoned with the word BOSS, came loping over. A tall man, with the air of a Harley Street physician, he looked surprisingly at ease in the muddy uniform of a site worker.

'Hail, Maecenas!' he greeted his visitor with an elaborate bow. 'We're away.'

'So I see. When did you assemble all of this?'

'They've been arriving all night.'

'That must have pleased Captain Legge.'

'Well,' smiled the architect grimly, 'it won't do the bugger any harm to have something solid to complain about for a change. Ah, Ted! This is Mr Ruggles who represents our lords and masters.'

'Good morning, sir.' The thick-set man who had joined them had a bonecrushing handshake and a pair of cold eyes that scarcely reinforced the polite greeting. 'The grade surveyors are just double-checking the angles of the outer canal,' he added.

The architect nodded. 'And the canteens?'

'All up and running.'

'Good man,' Gervase Yeatley-Smith said. 'That's a first class chap,' he added after the other had moved away. 'He's been with me from the beginning. Started as a builder's labourer, now he sends his son to Ampleforth. This place will be a monument to an age that can produce men like him.'

And us, they both thought companionably, as a series of yellow monsters trundled past on giant caterpillar tracks.

'Where will the campanile stand?' Henry Ruggles asked, fascinated by the havoc below them where an explosion the other end of the massive site signalled the passing of an old gravel escarpment.

'Over there. By those trees. There's a good solid base there.'

'And the church?'

'We're standing in the nave. The dome will be one hundred and ten feet above your head.'

Henry Ruggles stared up into the blue sky with its occasional wisps of cloud. 'It's hard to imagine,' he said.

'I expect that's what Pope Julius said to Michelangelo,' smiled the architect. 'This is pioneering work. We'll need the second instalment by the end of next week,' he added in a conversational tone.

The older man nodded. 'Don't worry,' he said. 'It'll be there. But remember that my clients want to see a return on their investment soon, and we can't start selling till the punters can see something concrete.'

'An unfortunate choice of words,' said Yeatley-Smith drily. 'There'll be no concrete here above ground. Only Forest of Dean bricks, good clean lime mortar and the finest Portland stone. I've just come from the quarry we've re-opened. They're working round the clock in four shifts to ensure maximum speed. Your clients can be selling by Christmas for occupancy in twelve months.'

Henry Ruggles ran his finger over his upper lip. 'And the first showhouse?'

Yeatley-Smith checked his diary. 'November twenty-fourth is the day the carpets go down. Say the twenty-sixth, that's a Saturday.'

'You're a great man,' said the lawyer.

'Just keep the money flowing in,' replied the architect. 'That's what keeps the show on the road.'

Later, standing by himself on a little knoll, Henry Ruggles took a last look round at the frenzied scene. For half a mile in both directions the mass of machines and men ground this way and that. Tall poles had been erected and, in his mind, he could begin to imagine the towers, pinnacles, domes and spires of this great enterprise. He was surprised to find tears trickling down his cheeks. No child in a sandpit could have experienced a greater sense of personal pride. Suddenly he realized he was very hot. In reaching to undo his tie, he caught sight of his wristwatch and started. It was already three o'clock. He had been due back at the office by lunchtime and he hurried back, through the groaning leviathans, conscious of the curious glances of sweating workmen. As soon as he reached his car he checked the telephone and found that it had logged eleven calls. Quickly he keyed the number of his secretary's direct line.

'Kenneth?'

'Oh, there you are, Mr Ruggles,' came an anxious reply. 'I've been trying to get you. Are you nearly here?'

'No, I'm sorry. I've been seriously delayed.'

'You have an appointment with Colonel Chesterfield in ten minutes.'

There was a note almost of panic in his aide's voice.

'That's all right,' Henry said calmly. 'Tell Mr Robin to stand in for me.'

'He's not here, sir. He went out unexpectedly.'

'What about Mr Bryce?'

'Yes. He's here.'

'Well, tell him to cope. Explain that my car broke down.' He rang off and, yielding to an overwhelming urge, took off his jacket and walked back towards the excavations.

Chapter 17

'Dear Tim, I haven't returned your calls because I don't want to see you again. It hasn't worked and I don't want to prolong the pain we would otherwise cause each other. I loved the flowers but please don't send any more. And don't write, I shall only return it unopened. With love, Flora'

Tim was re-reading this, his mouth dry from shock, when he heard that he was to stand in for his Senior Partner with, of all people, Colonel Chesterfield.

'Conference Room four, in ten minutes. Is that all right for you?'

'Yes, yes, Kenneth,' he answered mechanically. 'Put the papers on the table. I'll come straight in to run through them as best I can.'

He debated having a quick drink and decided against it. The Colonel would not be impressed by smelling whisky on his breath on a hot afternoon. He had hardly marched into the room and picked up the papers before the Colonel was ushered in with ceremonial pomp.

'I was expecting Ruggles,' he said abruptly, 'but I presume you know all about it.'

'I'm afraid his car has broken down,' said Tim apologetically.

'Well what does he expect, running that old

warhorse? He could get a new one like mine on what I pay him, I imagine.'

Tim smiled. The Senior Partner's car, a green and grey Rolls, was nearly forty years old and something of a joke in the office. It was popularly supposed that he'd accepted it from a grateful client and kept it out of a sentimental attachment. It certainly won no prizes for economy.

'You've read the papers?'

'A glance,' said Tim, gesturing at the thick pile of correspondence.

'No, no. The morning papers. This business of my tenants in Chesterfield Square is all over the *Express* and the *Independent*. Heartless landlord, unacceptable face of capitalism, total failure of legislation yet again. All that sort of thing.'

'Oh?'

'Yes, yes. That's those bloody sharks at Gallowglass of course. They think they can embarrass me, I suppose.' The Colonel showed his remaining teeth in what was almost a snarl. 'But it'll backfire. Because taking a firm line with these people will bring the others into line. You'll see.'

Tim nodded. It was probably true. 'What would you like us to do?'

'Issue immediate notices to quit to the two old biddies. If you've done your homework, you'll see that Counsel advised that their particular leases don't give them any protection. At least my uncle got something right for once. Not even this bloody Government could muck that up.'

'Mrs Lubbock and Miss Ingram?' checked Tim, writing as he spoke.

'That's them. That'll give them something to squawk about, I dare say.'

'I know Mr Ruggles wanted to talk to you about the political implications. It's rather a delicate moment, isn't it, with the new legislation?'

'Well thank God he's not here then,' said the Colonel. 'Where's that man with the tea?'

Tim pressed the bell beside his chair.

'On second thoughts,' said his client, 'I think I'll go for a large Scotch. I've just had rather an energetic lunchtime, if you know what I mean.' He smiled wolfishly and winked at Tim. 'You'd better have some yourself. You look as white as a sheet,' the Colonel went on, wiping something from his nose.

Tim stared at him, frozen with the thought of Flora pinned beneath this purple, sagging old man, giving him the use of her body to pay her debts.

'Take a tip from me,' the Colonel continued remorselessly, 'stick with the young girls. They keep you up to the mark, I can tell you.'

Tim forced a smile, as the steward backed into the room, balancing a tray of tea and cake.

'You're very lucky,' he said.

'Lucky?'

'Mrs Knox.'

The Colonel shot him a calculating glance. 'Fancied her, did you?'

'She was an excellent witness,' replied Tim coolly.

The Colonel waited till the door had closed again. 'She's a hot little number,' he confided. 'Really enjoys her work.' He licked his lips. Under the table, Tim's fists were clenched. The steward returned with the Colonel's whisky and Tim shook his head at the man's silent questioning offer of some for him.

'Very wise,' said the Colonel, taking a deep gulp from his glass. 'My doctor's always saying I should stick to wine during the day.' Suddenly he stood up.

'Well,' he said. 'That's it. Get on with it and damn the repercussions. I want them out in a month.'

'I'm sure they'll offer a compromise.'

'No compromise,' snapped the other. 'I'm going to make an example of them. Don't waste my time on that. It's time we had a little discipline in Chesterfield Square.' He paused then laughed uproariously. 'Yes,' he repeated, 'a little discipline does no-one any harm. When you get to my age, my boy, you'll see what I mean.'

After he had left, Tim changed his mind and ordered some whisky before reading Flora's letter again. It was entirely his own fault. He knew that well enough. He was clear-sighted enough to realize that she had begun to love him. The very fact that he had not been seriously disturbed by her continuing with the Colonel despite token protests had made him doubt his feelings for her. But whenever he had wanted to say more, to confess his own increasing need for her company, for her smile, for her touch, he had felt a matching interior withdrawal, almost an antagonism towards her. And now she had withdrawn completely. And in terms that he knew were final. Nothing about her had even suggested that she was given to making gestures. Was he a little relieved?

'No!' he shouted out loud, slamming down his empty glass, and beating his knee with his fist, no, he was not. What did he care for Laura Ingram's opinion, or any other blasted snob? It wouldn't even have helped to have thrown the scalding tea into the wrinkled sunburnt face of Flora's tormentor. It was hardly his fault, the old brute. But if Tim had asked her to live with him, even to marry him, would he not then have regretted it? He thought of ordering some more whisky. Instead, he rang down to Mordaunt, the litigation manager, and turned his mind reluctantly to issuing the necessary writs.

'Miss Laura Ingram is here to see you.' One of the receptionists had stuck her head round the door. 'She hasn't got an appointment.'

'Show her in.' He was too tired to care. No doubt she wanted some more money to pay her dressmaker. And why not? What else was he there for? He stood up when she stepped cautiously into his room, an unusually exotic figure in his mundane surroundings, in a swirling scarlet and mauve Pucci trouser suit tucked into red leather boots.

'I'm so sorry to appear without an appointment,' she said, shaking his hand, 'but I was passing and wanted to ask you for some advice.' She sat down in the chair he had indicated. 'I did tell them not to bother you if you were busy.'

'How may I help?' His attempt at a smile was not convincing. How could a girl like this understand the pressures of Flora's lonely fight against poverty? He had no sooner thought this than he realized its injustice. However much he loved Flora now that she had rejected him, he was not entirely blind to the fact that her debts were her own responsibility, and her methods of repaying them something less than ideal. Laura was guilty of little more than having a rich grandfather, and an easy line in hauteur. He decided to make an effort and gave her a second, and warmer, smile. 'Is it about money?'

She laughed. 'Poor you. You must have a very jaundiced view of all the Ingrams,' she said. 'I expect we're all in here off and on, demanding more cash.'

He grinned. It was very near the truth. 'But?'

'But. There is a but. I actually want less money and more to do. I feel I'm being turned into a vegetable by all these cheques you keep sending.' A very decorative vegetable, he couldn't help thinking, but one with thorns. 'I'd like to invest in something. I haven't quite thought what yet. I just wondered if I'm right to believe I could . . .' Her voice tailed away.

'Buy yourself a job?'

'Well,' she said uncertainly, 'put like that . . .'

'I think it's a good idea,' he said soothingly. 'But what are you interested in?'

'Horses. Discotheques. Lingerie. I'm only joking!' she said, laughing at his expression. 'I'm afraid I'm really only interested in something that will be a success. That means something for which there is a market. And that means something where there's a gap, a sort of need. Do you see?'

He was nodding thoughtfully. 'And?'

'And I wondered about light engineering? Perhaps aviation components? That must be a growth area?'

'Where do you pick up all this jargon?'

'Cosmopolitan. Where else?' she said sarcastically. She stood up. She had achieved all she wanted at this stage, which was to remind him of her existence, and try to sow a few favourable impressions. Time to quit while she was ahead. It would do no good to show irritation at his infuriating preconceptions. 'I mustn't take up too much of your time. Will you think about it?'

'I certainly will,' he said, relieved that she was going so soon. 'I think it's a very imaginative idea.' She was, in fact, the first member of her family to consider direct investment in the twelve years he had dealt with them.

Left alone, his thoughts reverted to Flora. Surely there was some way he could change her mind. But then, had he changed his? Or would they just be reverting to the same impasse? He decided he would have some whisky after all.

'I met an admirer of yours today,' murmured the Colonel much later, as he was ramming himself rather half-heartedly into Flora's listless flesh. She gazed up at him in uncomprehending torpor. Twice in one day was worse than she could ever have imagined.

'Yes,' he said, 'young Bryce. He was positively slavering.' The violent contraction of her body took him by surprise, delivering an orgasm that was as delightful to the Colonel as it was unwelcome to Flora.

'My word,' he muttered once he had recovered. 'Now I know what to talk about in future!' He groaned as he stretched out for a handkerchief. 'But you stick to me,' he added. 'I don't want to catch the clap again at my age.'

Chapter 18

With Robin's dubious loan returned so swiftly, Tim felt no need to speak to Henry or reveal that Judy, the junior financial specialist, had spotted the misdemeanour. In any event, his time was fully taken up preparing Dapper's case which was due to come before the magistrates for its preliminaries. The sale at Garrisons had netted nearly four hundred thousand pounds after commission thanks to fierce competition for a pretty pair of Nasmyth landscapes among the gloomy faces of Gumbys past. But that money would not be paid for at least a month and was now the subject of a separate court order in favour of Perry's Bank.

'You should be paying for this out of your own pocket,' Robin had snarled when informed that his father had sanctioned Tim's continued representation of Dapper.

Instead of borrowing the money from the Clients' Account? was the reply that Tim had had great difficulty in restraining.

Twice he telephoned Flora, and twice she spoke to him rationally, calmly, kindly, explaining that she did not wish to be further involved with him either as lover or even as friend, his final despairing offer of compromise.

If, however, he could have seen her sad white face, as she listened for a few extra moments to the dialling tone after he had finally rung off, the involuntary heaving of her shoulders as she rolled over sideways on to the green-quilted bed, hugging a pillow to her in a vain attempt to stifle the pain, he would not have been so bitter at the ease with which she appeared to exclude him.

As she cradled the pillow to her breasts, some acrid odour rose, reminding her of the bed's other regular occupant. The Colonel! Suddenly she stood up.

I've had enough, she thought. If I can give up Tim, I can certainly give up the Colonel. Within ten minutes, she had swept such few belongings as were hers into a sagging tartan suitcase and almost ran down the stairs in her eagerness to turn resolve into action. She hadn't the faintest idea where she was going. She did know that Scrymgeour Square, with its depraved mixture of luxury and humiliation, was no longer part of her life.

At the bottom of the stairs, she surprised the spindly couple below setting off for a walk in the Square gardens.

'Goodbye,' she said. 'I'm off!'

The woman looked sourly away while the man politely made to raise his little grey hat. Flora was halfway to Heathrow in a taxi before she remembered she had left her passport in the dressing table drawer. With a shrug, she ordered the driver to turn round and take her to King's Cross instead. 'Tomintoul here I come,' she sighed aloud, and started to cry again.

The next two weeks were the hottest ever recorded in London in June. The whole city steamed as a remorseless sun baked the buildings. The streets were full of the stink of human and mechanized waste. Men abandoned their stifling suits, revealing crumpled shirts, and the shops sold out of cotton trousers while women blossomed into a brilliant array of flowered blouses. The Underground became almost unusable as the heat of the trains mixed with that of the streets. Everyone who could had fled to the countryside.

Perky stared at her bedhead, blinking through the sweat that ran down between her eyes. The board was upholstered in a crimson silk brocade, piped with a plain matching satin. She had found the materials quite by chance, in a little shop off Mortimer Street. There had been just enough to cover the bed and the Louis Seize armchair that sat ready by the bathroom door to receive the day's discarded clothes. It was just beginning to show some signs of wear, a little shine here, some shredding at the base there.

It was good to have a chance to review her household arrangements. She had long coveted a heavy gilded base in Mallett's. All it needed was one of those inlaid marble mosaic tops and then it would fit perfectly into the alcove to the left of the front door. She could put her terracotta bust of Marie Antoinette on it, with the Genoese bronze tigers on either side. It would be quite spectacular.

By the sound of it, Max would soon collapse heavily on top of her. She could feel the heat of his quickened gasps on the back of her neck, and his hands were tightening painfully on her breasts. Then they could talk tables. She gave a little wiggle and was rewarded by a convulsive groan. It was like playing snakes and ladders. If that happy groan was something of a ladder, it was immediately followed by a serious snake, when the whole of Max's weight drove her face precipitously into the bedhead.

'Oh Perky,' he sighed as she fought for breath. 'Oh darling.' Definitely time for tables!

'Max,' she said when he had recovered and was lying beside her half asleep.

'Yes, you gorgeous creature.'

'Can we go shopping later?'

There was a long, long silence. Max's face held no expression, his eyelids firmly closed. Perky watched him with a half smile.

But if his outward mien was one of calm, inside all was curdling confusion – anger, fear, pride and lust, churning about like mental vomit. What his daughter had said was true. Henry Ruggles sent him twelve and a half thousand punctually on the fifth of each month, just for his personal expenditure. Since all his household bills, both in London and down at Milston, were paid through the Estate Office, and all his tax affairs were settled without reference to him by Ruggles, Cavendish & Bryce, it had used to be something of a struggle to find ways of spending this. But now, thanks to Perky, he was seriously in debt to his bank.

Idly she stroked his matted hair and he shifted uneasily, as if her touch was unwelcome. His recent request for an extra payment to clear his growing overdraft had been met with a strangely abrupt refusal from Henry Ruggles. In the past, such payments had often come through automatically. Nearly a whole year's income decorated this woman's body and already she was talking about more! And yet . . .

His dark brows wrinkled together in an involuntary rictus of self-pity.

'What is it?' she asked softly, bending over to tickle his ear with her tongue.

He sat up abruptly. 'What is it that you need now?' he said aggressively, though pulling her naked body close to his as if in contradiction of his mutinous tone.

'Come with me to Bond Street and I'll show you.'

Bond Street! He was beginning to long for the village store in Milston, with its cosy stock of postcards and the inexpensive but colourful bottles of boiled sweets. He climbed off the bed and stalked over to the window, peering through its drawn curtains on to the baking cobbles in the little street below.

'I'm sorry,' he said. 'It's difficult for me to say this. But I think I shall have to withdraw from your hospitality for the moment. I am rather short of funds.'

Perky, her moist torso brilliantly spotlit by a shaft of afternoon sun, the beads of sweat glittering so that she momentarily appeared to be spangled with tiny gems, smiled up at his broad back matted with damp grey hair. She knew he was behaving with deliberate rectitude in the hope that she would soften and entertain him for the sake of his own undoubted attractions.

'I will await that moment with great eagerness,' she said. No man had ever returned to her after the humiliation of admitting that her price was too steep. This was goodbye and she was already playing it so as to cushion the blow for him as best she could.

'But Perky!' His eyes were pleading, and he strode back to the bed, sank down and laid his face against her dripping flank. 'Think of what I've spent on you.'

She took his head in both her hands, raised it towards her and kissed him long and tenderly, first on the lips, and then on both his eyes.

'I prefer,' she whispered softly, 'to think of what you've spent in me.'

At the thought of losing her, his whole body tautened as if in the embrace of death, and she pulled him up to her and in. Splashed by his tears, she watched his final moments as her hand snaked round and with a painful gasp he thrust her backwards with the strength of his paroxysm.

Later, repainting her nails, she glanced at herself in the mirror and noted, for the first time, an infinitesimal line that ran down the centre of her forehead like a hairline crack.

Chapter 19

The Magistrates' Court was packed for Dapper's preliminary hearing. It was to be something of a formality and Gilles de Wirth, nearing the end of his two-year secondment overseeing Perry's Bank on behalf of his main board in Geneva, had almost decided not to bother attending, even though it had been his decision that Perry's lay a complaint against Dapper within ten minutes of Tim leaving the Chairman the morning of his appointment.

In the end, the voyeuristic lure of watching someone else struggling in the web brought his chauffeur-driven Daimler to rest a hundred yards short of the courthouse. He sat calmly in the back of the car, observing with distaste the untidiness of the people hurrying to work, while his driver ran to buy him a copy of *The Times*. This was more for a prop than for information, since he had been at his desk since dawn, scanning the world's markets on the various screens linked to the Bank's mainframe. Folding it neatly under his arm, he sauntered into the dour old-fashioned building with its flaking green paint and shabby metal benches. He nodded at Tim who was standing leafing through some papers with a thin woman beside him, perhaps his assistant, talking into a mobile telephone. Dapper, a taut smile slashed across his face, was smoking the last inch of a Turkish cigarette, which, as Gilles watched, he flicked accurately out of the open window behind him.

The prosecutor was to be Ted Ridley, the Treasury silk, but since he was finishing a case at the Old Bailey, his junior, Rebecca Pasley-Tyler, was handling the day's proceedings. She waved at Gilles and came across with Smith, the Treasury solicitor, with whom Gilles had spent most of two days preparing the case.

'Everything in order?' he asked perfunctorily.

The prosecuting solicitor nodded, adding, 'Rather a lot of Press for some reason.'

Gilles raised his eyebrows. 'I thought they didn't usually bother with preliminary hearings.'

'They don't,' sniffed the other. 'I think they've been lured here as a tactic to discomfit the bank.'

Gilles frowned. This was not welcome news. It was precisely the argument advanced by Sir Robert that he had had to overcome in pressing for immediate prosecution.

'Well – keep it short,' he said after a moment's thought. 'I'll get our public relations people to mount a spoiler before the main trial.' His companions appeared not to have heard – they were, after all, working for the Crown, not for Perry's Bank.

Somewhere a shrill bell announced the approach of ten o'clock and people began drifting in to their allotted places, Dapper stepping nimbly into the dock with the faint smile still precariously in position.

'And so,' said Rebecca after outlining the simple facts of the case, that Dapper had signed an undertaking pledging the proceeds of any sales to the bank, that he had received a sum in advance, and that notwithstanding his undertaking, he had paid the money direct to the Mount Street Casino with the intention of defrauding the Bank, since he knew that he would not then be able to pay off his debts to them.

'It is the Crown's contention that in doing so he committed a fraudulent conversion of funds which he knowingly held in trust for Perry's Bank.' She sat down, amid much scribbling of journalistic pencils. 'We ask for a Committal,' she added, half rising in her seat as an afterthought.

The three magistrates, an enormously fat Chairman with a pince-nez, flanked by two severe ladies, one in checks, the other in lavender blue, huddled together like contestants in a television quiz.

The Chairman mopped his brow and turned courteously to Tim. 'No doubt your client wishes to reserve his defence for the trial?'

Tim stood and smiled back with equal courtesy. 'On the contrary, your honour. Mr Gumby, confident that there is no case to answer, wishes the case to be heard summarily here,' adding helpfully, when he saw the magistrate's perplexed frown, 'forthwith.'

There was an excited buzz round the room.

'Here?' echoed the old man anxiously. 'Forthwith?'

'Yes, indeed,' emphasized Tim, agreeably aware of Rebecca Pasley-Tyler's open-mouthed consternation. 'As is his right, with the Bench's acquiescence.'

'I see.' The magistrate was looking round for the Clerk, but the latter, a young man with a foxy moustache, was thumbing through a thick red volume with some show of confusion.

'I must protest.' Rebecca was on her feet now. 'This is totally unexpected and a very unusual way of proceeding.'

'Mr Bryce?' The magistrate turned back, hoping perhaps to be spared this public dilemma.

'Our case is,' Tim spoke loudly and clearly, having spotted the hearing aid in the check lady's right ear, 'that my client has been quite unjustifiably accused of a crime which never took place. His good name has been seriously impugned – something for which he will in due course be seeking redress in a separate civil action. Meantime, every day that this charge remains extant, his reputation continues to suffer. Since it is our contention that the case can be simply and swiftly resolved today, I would ask the Bench to agree, as is their undoubted right, to hear the case and deal with it summarily, subject only of course,' he bowed deeply, 'to their equal right to refer sentencing to a higher court in the event of a conviction, if they in their wisdom so choose.'

The magistrate shook his head as if to loosen some foreign body unexpectedly lodged therein. 'I *see*,' he said again. 'Mr Tricker?'

The clerk, still clutching his thick volume, advanced to the magistrates' dais, his little eyes darting about anxiously.

'Is what Mr Bryce says correct?'

The clerk bowed low. 'Yes, your honour. The Bench may choose to hear the case summarily if the defendant so wishes. It is however highly irregular.'

'Highly irregular!' interrupted Smith, the Treasury solicitor, unwisely rising in his seat. 'Unheard of, I should say.'

Perhaps the Chairman was unaware that this new champion in the lists was speaking from the solicitors' table, or perhaps he had himself suffered at the hands of Perry's Bank. Certainly this interruption decided the issue, because after ten seconds of silent glowering at Smith, he rapped the table and said,

'Very well. Miss Parsley-Taylor, proceed with your case.'

'But, your honour . . .'

'We have reached our decision,' he snapped back. 'Kindly proceed.'

'May I ask the Court's indulgence of an adjournment. I am led in this case by my learned colleague Mr Ridley. He is currently appearing before the Lord Chief Justice at the Old Bailey, but I should like his advice before proceeding.'

'Mr Bryce?'

'Well, your honour,' said Tim. 'My client has already waited some time for the chance to clear his name of this grievous accusation. The Crown chose this date. If they have grander things to do,' his tone was especially silken, 'then they should either abandon this prosecution, or proceed immediately.'

'I entirely agree.' This time the magistrate was sure of his ground. 'If Mr Ridley is too busy to be bothered with us, you will have to do your best.' He took out a fountain pen, unscrewed its top, and held it poised expectantly, the image of attentive concentration.

Rebecca shrugged hopelessly. Smith passed a note to Gilles. It read, 'We will need Sir Robert *immediately*.' Gilles read it and hurried from the room.

The next hour was spent with Rebecca painstakingly explaining to the Court the extent of Dapper's dealings with the Bank and the problems relating to the now worthless Sarti shares lodged with the Bank in accordance with the conditions attached to their releasing the deeds to the property Dapper had sold to the dead industrialist.

'Let me get this right,' said the magistrate. 'The defendant owed Perry's Bank roughly six hundred thousand pounds. This was made up of a farm overdraft of just under half a million secured against the deeds of Gumby-in-the-Vale, and a private unsecured overdraft of almost a hundred and twenty thousand pounds?'

'No,' said Rebecca. 'The private overdraft *had* been unsecured. But the defendant visited the bank last autumn and signed the document you have in front of you – no, not the summons, yes, that one – which specifically secures the contents of Gumby-in-the-Vale against both accounts, as well as introducing a general charge against the defendant's assets wheresoever arising in favour of the Bank.'

The old magistrate blinked. 'Let me try again,' he said. 'So he sold his house, eleven subsidiary cottages and fourteen hundred acres of land to Mr Sarti and received in return Sarti shares then valued at just over three million pounds. These were lodged with Perry's.'

'Yes, your honour.' Rebecca's studied patience was all too audible. 'The contract price was originally for three point one million pounds, but it was subsequently amended to three point two three five million pounds, in return for which he accepted shares to that value as valued on the day of completion with reference to the price quoted that morning on the London Stock market.'

The two outer magistrates conferred behind their Chairman's back. Then the elder one whispered in his ear.

'Yes,' the Chairman said. 'My colleagues have raised an interesting point. Surely that meant the defendant had discharged his overdraft and was very substantially in credit?'

Rebecca shook her head. 'No, your honour.'

'No?'

'No. The Bank received the shares as required by the terms under which they released the deeds to the property to the conveyancers who were transferring title to Mr Sarti. But they received the share certificates, in place of the deeds, as security against the loans.'

'But why weren't the loans paid off?'

'Because the Bank had no instructions from the defendant to sell the shares.'

The magistrate leant forward and put his pen down with a snap. 'You mean that those were the shares which were subsequently suspended and are now valueless?'

'Yes, your honour.'

The old man sighed and turned to look at first one colleague and then the other. There was no doubting his train of thought: Here was a man who had to sell his home to satisfy his bank, only to find that some further scandal in the City had not only ruined him but also laid him open to vindictive persecution by a company who had been only too happy to lend him large sums without security in the palmy days of his prosperity.

Smith scribbled another note to Gilles, who had returned accompanied by Sir Robert. 'I don't think he likes banks.' There was no reply, Gilles being too conscious of the heavy breathing of his furious superior, summoned precipitously to the Court as he was dressing to drive down to Goodwood.

'And will we hear evidence from the Bank in question?'

'Yes indeed,' Rebecca bowed. 'I am now calling Sir Robert Mackay, the Chairman of Perry's, who has cancelled a pressing engagement to join us.'

'Very good of him, I'm sure,' sniffed the magistrate, as the angry banker walked swiftly into the witness box and took the oath. Once the basic facts had been elicited, it was Tim's turn to cross-examine.

'Good morning, Sir Robert,' he said cheerfully. The other nodded silently. 'I want you to tell the Court the circumstances under which my client signed the undertaking.'

'Well.' Sir Robert shifted uneasily under Tim's steady gaze. 'He came to see me last autumn.'

'At his request?'

'No. I telephoned him myself.'

'Do you deal with all the clients yourself?'

'Of course not. Mr Gumby is by way of being a personal friend.'

'Indeed?' Tim raised his eyebrows and exchanged a significant look with the old magistrate. 'A personal *friend*?' After the briefest of pauses, he continued, 'And why did you tell him you wanted to see him?'

'Why?'

'Yes – why?'

The banker narrowed his eyes and awkwardly fingered his buttonhole, an inappropriately gaudy orchid.

'Isn't it a fact,' said Tim, 'that he was there because you asked him to lunch with no intimation that business was to be discussed?'

'Yes. That may well be so.'

'Isn't it also a fact that at no point in any of his dealings has my client transacted any business at your bank without being accompanied and advised by someone from my firm?'

'I really wouldn't know.'

'If necessary I will,' Tim brandished a thick wad of notes, 'take the Court through every appointment made by my client over the past twenty years since he achieved his majority. It will save all our time if you are prepared to concede that what I say is true.'

There was a long silence, and then the banker nodded. 'If you say so,' he said.

'I do,' said Tim. 'And it was, therefore, unique and against all established practice for you, my client's *personal* friend, to give him a paper to sign about which he had no independent advice other than from you, as I say, his personal friend.'

This time the silence was intense.

'And so,' Tim was again on his feet in the late afternoon, 'rather than proceeding with the defence, I would ask the Court to rule today that no case has been made out for my client to answer. He was a man of considerable means, now much reduced as the victim of another's fraud. He was inveigled by the Chairman of the powerful institution with whom his family have banked for over three hundred years, a man whom he trusted as a friend, to sign a piece of paper which was imperfectly explained to him and which, had he been given the chance to receive advice as was the invariable custom and practice on all contracts made between him and Perry's Bank, would never have been signed. On the basis of this legerdemain, he is now being prosecuted as a common criminal while struggling to clear his debts. These arose solely because the shares which he entirely properly lodged with the Bank, far in excess of his indebtedness, lost their value before they could be converted into cash. I can never remember,' Tim consciously swelled his voice to echo what he hoped to be the magistrates' personal feelings, 'a more infamous prosecution, more shoddily prepared, or more vindictively pursued, launched moreover by a corporation whose Chairman has the effrontery to claim his victim as a "personal friend". I would ask the Bench to dismiss this case with costs.'

'It seems to be your forte,' said Robin with a sneer at the office meeting that evening, 'to get the guilty off their hooks.'

Tim shrugged and drained his whisky.

'I suppose you realize Perry's will hold this against us,' his partner continued.

'Come, come,' said Henry, patting his son's sleeve. 'If the Bench dismissed the case, it follows that Dapper was innocent. I don't think he'll have any more cheques returned for a little while.'

'*With* costs,' added Tim slyly.

'Oh yes,' shouted Robin. 'You'll get paid. It's the only Gumby bill that will be paid, you see. All that's happened is you've delayed the inevitable and damaged our relations with one of the major clearing banks into the bargain.'

'If,' retorted Tim, 'you had alerted me to his arrest as was your absolute duty, he would probably never have been charged.' Robin's face seemed actually to swell as angry blood churned into its arteries, turning his complexion from a sullen mauve into a furnace of clashing crimsons.

'You little shit!' he bellowed. 'I've a good mind to smash your silly nose in.' He stood up, but his father seized his arm.

'Robin! What is the matter with you?' The old lawyer's face seemed grey beside his bull-like child. Tim watched them both with detached interest.

'If I am a little shit,' he said thoughtfully, 'then you must be a truly colossal turd. Because it's you who is clogging up the system. Have you told your father about your rather individual approach to the money held by us in the Clients' Account?'

Such was the silence that followed this remark that they could all distinctly hear the office steward's heavy breathing from where he stood, outside in the corridor, eagerly listening to the loudest row among his employers in thirty years.

'What does he mean?' The balance of power had shifted very suddenly. Henry's voice was no longer that of a fond parent. Robin sank back into his chair, staring at Tim. '*What does he mean?*'

In fact, Tim had never seen this side of his senior partner before. The little man was positively fizzing with energy. He shook his son's shoulder.

'I borrowed some money overnight when I hadn't got my cheque book,' said Robin slowly. 'It's all right,' he added in a more confident tone, 'I paid it straight back the following morning. Heaven knows how this little creep found out.'

'Since I am at least six inches taller than you,' said Tim, 'I suggest you should rethink your obsession with my size. It reflects rather poorly on your eyesight. Although I do concede a contest based on waistlines.'

'Please,' said Henry. 'This sort of childishness does not advance our business interests. You, Robin,' he said, turning on his son, 'have clearly made a complete and embarrassing fool of yourself, to put it no stronger. You, indeed both of us, are lucky that Tim is a good partner, in every way. I'm sure we can all agree to end this matter here and now.' He glanced at Tim, a look both challenging and yet beseeching. Tim nodded. 'Good. Now I should like to be left alone with Tim to deal with other matters, so perhaps you should go down and sort out our claim for costs in the Gumby hearing.'

Robin stood up, nodded to his father, and walked slowly out of the room, without a glance at Tim. As he reached the door, he paused almost as if he was intending to return to the battle. But it was only a tiny pause, and then the door closed behind him.

The two others sat in silence for several minutes, neither knowing how best to continue.

'What news of the Colonel's tenants?' asked Tim eventually of his senior partner.

Henry smiled. 'They've caved in. Gallowglass have conceded our case. It's just a question of getting the Colonel to halt the evictions. He's a cunning old bird. I don't think he'll press it now the rent's been paid. He's rather down in the dumps over something. He just told me to handle it in my own way. He's off to Scotland at the end of the month.'

On this note, the meeting ended. When Tim got back to his office, he found, to his great surprise, Laura sitting in the armchair by the filing cabinet, reading his copy of the *Daily Mail*.

'Hello,' he said, feeling his face stiffen at the sight of her self-confident expression. 'What now?'

'I'm back again,' she said. Her throat was constricted with nerves, so that her voice sounded unnatural even to her. Why did he always glower so? 'I think I've found the perfect firm.'

Immediately he remembered. Something about investing to find herself an occupation. 'Oh good.' He was still seething about Robin. Why couldn't he have married this woman, and kept her out of the way?

'It's called Cholmondeley Associates.' It would be, he thought sourly. 'They've been developing an individual in-flight telecommunications system and they think they've cracked the problem of interference with the plane's systems.'

'But?'

'But they've hit serious cash flow problems.'

Not an Ingram problem.

'How much do you know about precision engineering?'

'Not much,' she conceded. Perhaps she was just obsessed with this man. How can you love a tailor's dummy who you've hardly ever spoken to, and who glares at you when you beard him in his lair? And yet she was longing to kiss him, to tell him how much she admired his quiet and self-effacing vigour.

'How did you hear of them?'

'The managing director is the brother of a friend of mine.'

He weighed up the idea. She seemed rather young to become the City's newest takeover baron. And yet, she certainly had the money. There would be twenty, thirty, thriving small companies like this who would turn any hoop for a cash injection of a couple of million. She could increase her income and find an outlet for her energies. Rather them than me, was his uncharitable judgement of working alongside an inexperienced partner with her sort of looks. She really was very beautiful. There was a sheen to her skin which made her seem to glow. And her lips! It was a pity, he thought, that she was so arrogant with it. But perhaps that was to be expected. What on earth was this dewy expression meant to signify?

'It's a very interesting proposition,' he said, making up his mind not to discourage her simply because he found her so infuriating. 'It would need the Trustees' support of course, but I think they would be keen on the idea. Do you realize,' he went on, relenting a little now in the warmth of her smile, 'that you are the first of all the beneficiaries to suggest something so positive?'

She was positively beaming. 'So? What about it?' She paused and looked at him. What could have caused that wariness, that constant flicker of withdrawal that spoilt his looks so?

'I'll talk to our research expert,' he said. 'We've got this young graduate who specializes in analysing company prospects. Give me a couple of days.' He got up and walked back to the door. He felt suddenly tired, his head full of thoughts of Flora. He wanted to be left alone. 'And I'll speak to Henry.'

She stood up, trying not to show her chagrin at being dismissed so quickly. 'Thank you,' she said. 'Do you still go to the opera?'

'No,' he said, and put out his hand. 'I'll let you know what we come up with.'

After she had left, he sat down behind his desk and from the very back of a drawer he took out a little brown envelope. It was labelled 'Material'. Carefully he slit it open, and withdrew a folded square of beige silk the size of a large pocket handkerchief. With a swift, practised movement, he drew it to his face, breathing in deeply as he did so. But there remained now only the slightest hint of Flora's natural fragrance; already this final vestige of her power over him was beginning to lose its power. Yet he stayed there, stifled with nostalgia, as beyond his window the merciless summer sun began at last to sink behind the massive spire of St Simeon.

Chapter 20

'HIS ROYAL HIGHNESS THE PRINCE ARTHUR!'

The toastmaster, in scarlet livery, was seriously testing his lungs. Many heads swivelled to log the entry of their errant Prince, boulevardier to the backstreets of Europe, as he acknowledged Lady Woodchester's curtsy, itself a tribute to the reinforced elastic and Heath Robinson ingenuity of her corsetier.

Lady Woodchester now gave three major parties each year – a soirée after the opening of the Chelsea Flower Show, this the annual ball on the third night of glorious Goodwood, and finally her Ghillies' Ball, held since acquiring the thirty square miles of mixed rockery and heather garden that made up the Strathdhui estate in Banffshire. Each party had its traditional guest of honour, and tonight was Prince Arthur's turn, since Lord Woodchester regularly paid for the Prince's private orchestra.

'That's what I call a genuine civil list,' murmured Lord Sennowe, the Prince's elderly equerry, to Tim as they watched their hostess struggling to right herself after such an ambitious exertion. 'Oh look, I want to introduce you to an old friend of mine. Perky! Hi! Perky!' The old courtier waved his coloured handkerchief above the heads of the crowd so that several people stared at him before his quarry, sipping a glass of champagne by one of the pillars that supported the ballroom ceiling, saw him, put down her glass and waved back.

'You darling girl.' He beamed at her and embraced her warmly as she darted into his arms. 'Ah no! Not that!' He protested delightedly as she suddenly tickled his ribs. 'Not in front of my Boss!'

Tim, watching with his mouth open, took her proffered hand.

'My dear,' said the older man, 'this is my young friend Tim Bryce, Miss Metternich.'

Perky smiled at Tim, noting the dense black curls and the hesitant blue eyes. Not a patch on Dapper, she decided, but much more prosperous. In particular she liked the look of the diamond studs. She touched one.

'I like the look of these,' she said.

'Can't you two wait till my back's turned?' Lord Sennowe was positively elated at seeing her, and oblivious of Tim's increasing embarrassment. After all, they had only met half a dozen times in the bar at White's. Tim scarcely knew the old man. Perky, however, spotted his unease and immediately drew back and with easy tact found herself carried away by the slipstream that eddied in the Prince's wake.

'What a spectacular dress,' said Tim. The other slapped him on the back.

'A great lady,' he said with an emphasis assisted by draining a heavy tumbler of something sticky. 'And at seventeen the most beautiful girl I had ever seen. She came to stay with us down in Norfolk, you know. Stayed longer than she expected.' He winked at Tim. 'I'm too old for that sort of thing now. It's you young fellows' turn. Hi! You there!'

A startled waiter halted so abruptly that the glasses

on his tray rocked on their fragile stems. 'Any more Kummel?'

The man turned obediently and retreated into the crowd.

'DON'T FORGET THE ICE!' bellowed the old courtier at his disappearing back. 'Oh God! Now I've lost the Boss. He'll be belly-aching about something, I don't doubt.'

Tim, left alone, started pacing around the tall room to see if Flora was there. This he did every day – in the street, in the shops, even on the Underground. He could see Colonel Chesterfield sitting at a card table, apparently having an argument with his bridge partner, Jim Lubbock, the Minister. He could recognize various Ingrams, including Laura who was talking to a jubilant Dapper. But of Flora, there was no sign. He sighed.

'Oh *dear*!' said an amused voice at his side. 'Are things *that* bad?' He looked round to find Perky at his side again.

Before he could reply, she clutched his arm. 'Quick! I need your protection. Pretend you've asked me to dance.'

'So there you are!' Max Ingram had strode through a gaggle of debutantes and stood in front of them, hands on hips, his heavy eyebrows drawn together. He looked distinctly drunk.

'Do you know each other?' asked Perky, who had forgotten Tim's name.

'I think we ought to,' snapped Max, 'since this young man has had the impertinence to refuse to send me some of my own money.'

Tim stared. 'I have?'

'You or one of your dreary partners.'

'I'm very surprised to hear it.'

'So you should be. So was I. Now,' Max manoeuvred himself so as to exclude Tim while facing Perky, 'you and I are going to dance.'

'Oh Max,' sighed Perky, resting one hand on his arm, 'I wish I could, but I have put Tim off twice' (the name had miraculously returned) 'and now it really is his turn in the nightclub.'

'And a damned expensive club it is too,' snapped Max, 'where you're concerned.'

An uneasy silence was beginning to form around the little group. Lord Woodchester, happening to pass, put his arm round Max's shoulders.

'My dear fellow! The very chap I've been looking for. Is there any chance of luring you up to Strathdhui for a week in September?' He carried off his disgruntled guest leaving Tim and Perky alone in a vacuum as those around lost interest and reverted to their own preoccupations.

'So?' she said.

'So?' He felt at a loss.

'Are you going to dance with me or not?' She was taller than Flora, with none of her crack-toothed gamine charm. He surrendered.

'But of course.' He steered her towards the nightclub, oblivious of Laura's furious eyes watching them through the crowd.

But it was Flora whom he held as they danced, their faces fitfully splashed with the coloured lights, Flora whom he drove back to Chelsea, and Flora whose legs he felt wrapped tightly round his waist, just as it was Dapper's name she whispered as unaccustomed waves of emotion swept through Perky's ivory flesh.

'Well. That was a first,' she said ruefully as he woke her with a glass of fresh orange juice.

He smiled down at her. 'In that?'

'In that people usually pay me.'

'Oh.' It wasn't exactly the answer he had expected.

She reached up and squeezed his hand. 'Not in retrospect.'

He nodded, but added waspishly, 'And not at all in Dapper's case, I imagine!'

She was silent for a moment. 'You heard?'

He nodded again, and got in beside her, pulling her close to him.

'I've only ever spoken to him twice,' she said. 'That's what's so silly.'

Chapter 21

Down in Hampshire, men and machines were pushing the earth this way and that under the sweltering summer sun. Like some Titan's crossword puzzle, the prodigious excavations ran together in perfect symmetry, and now that the miles of shuttering had been satisfactorily filled with concrete, here and there brick walls began to rise in the foundations to give perspective to the whole.

Captain Legge, gloomily surveying his new neighbours through the telescope he had installed on his roof, muttered a salty oath, his only comfort being today's headline that another building society had closed its doors.

'At least the buggers won't be able to sell a sausage,' he remarked to his wife over lunch. 'It'll just be one gigantic folly. Perhaps,' his face brightened, 'perhaps they'll let us sail on the main canal?'

On the site, Gervase Yeatley-Smith was munching a sandwich while completing the full working drawing of the campanile's stringcourse.

'Any sign of Ruggles?' he asked Ted, his foreman, for the fourth time in an hour. The latter, engrossed in an airline-style luncheon box, made no reply.

Despite the heat opening deep fissures in the underlying clay, while reducing the chalky topsoil to a fine dust, they were ahead of schedule. With so many of their competitors out of the business altogether, the production of the stone quarries had also outdone all expectations and to the west of the site, guarded by floodlit razor-wire and half a dozen alsatian dogs, rose an impressive stockpile of masonry, some blocks rough-hewn, some dressed, but all ready to face the palatial buildings, as their inner walls rose towards the cloudless sky.

'I suppose there really is a market for this sort of thing?' said Ted unexpectedly, his mouth full of stilton.

The architect stared at him. 'That's not our problem,' he said. 'Our job is to build the thing so it doesn't fall down.'

The other chuckled. 'You know that only happened once.'

'Well, I don't want to have to go through that again,' said Gervase with a frown. 'Once was quite enough.'

There was a tap on the door.

'Come.'

The purple perspiring face of Henry Ruggles peered blinking in at the comparative darkness. He slumped down in an empty chair and loosened his tie. His collar was drenched and crumpled. 'This weather!' he said. 'I've never known anything like it.'

'Have you brought the cheque?' Gervase Yeatley-Smith had his priorities firmly in order.

'Yes, yes,' sighed the solicitor. 'Here's your money.' He passed over an envelope which the architect tore open, putting the cheque inside against another piece of paper lying among his drawings.

'It's over a million short,' he protested, looking up angrily at his employer.

'No, it's not,' contradicted the other. 'It's your last three invoices paid in full as per our schedule.'

'But we're ahead of the schedule, as you know.'

'Splendid. But our contract is very precise. There's no flexibility in the cash flow. It's no good my giving you a worthless cheque.' Henry smiled with all the confidence of a man working to a contract he has himself devised. 'The payments are planned to coincide with the funds available to my clients.'

Gervase stared at him, uncomfortably aware that his foreman was, in turn, watching him to see how he would react.

'But there's a hefty penalty clause if we fall behind.'

'Certainly,' beamed Henry. 'Because that would affect my clients' ability to market their houses.'

'But my sub-contractors,' protested the architect. 'They are expecting payment.'

'And no doubt they will get it on our next settlement day,' replied Henry imperturbably. 'Or you could pay them out of your advance fees. I'm sure your figures allow for that. Not,' he added, quickly, seeing the architect's face darkening with anger, 'that I wish to involve myself in how you run your business. You're doing splendidly, and I don't doubt there'll be a bonus at the end of the day if there are no hiccups.'

After he had gone, the two colleagues sat in silence.

'He's paid up handsomely so far,' said Ted, deciding that nothing was to be gained by encouraging Gervase's mood. 'I expect he's not given much rope by his clients.'

'Clients!' shouted the furious architect. 'I don't believe in his fucking clients. This is some sort of game as far as he is concerned. He's after glory, using my genius – that's Henry Ruggles for you. Damned parasite!'

The foreman shrugged. When Yeatley-Smith got into one of his tantrums, he preferred to be out and doing.

'I'll just go and check the fall on the main drainage,' he said. Reluctantly clapping on his helmet, he marched out into the furnace of the August sun, thinking longingly of his wife and children in their leafy northern suburb.

With Henry out of the office and Robin taking an extended holiday in Thailand, Tim was left in charge of the business. With the air conditioning turned full up, and his office curtains drawn against the glare, he was sitting at his desk indulging in an after-lunch glance at the papers. Not for the first time that day, his face was screwed up with an anxious frown. Something had been forgotten. But what? Suddenly he was startled by the jangling trill of his telephone.

'Yes?'

'Mr Bryce?' It was not a voice he recognized.

'Yes. Yes.'

'It's Julie. From finance. May I come and see you for a moment?'

'Of course. Come straight up.'

Surely Robin hadn't been pilfering again? Perhaps he shouldn't have revealed that he knew. Then he remembered. This, of course, was the girl who had been researching companies for Laura Ingram's venture. She came in, her nose painfully red from a summer cold.

'Would you like a cup of tea?' he said sympathetically.

She shook her head. 'I'd rather no-one knew I was here,' she said. Was she suffering from paranoia?

He put down his paper, and opened a notebook. 'Did you find anything interesting about that telephone company, Cholmondeley Whatsit?'

She stared past him, obviously still uncertain how to broach her subject.

He tried a different tack. 'Is it Robin again?'

She shook her head, then thrust a computer sheet in front of him. He recognized it immediately as the Ingram Trust July monthly return. He studied it attentively.

'It looks all right to me,' he said at last. 'The normal income distributions. Max Ingram was complaining the other day he had been refused an extra payment. There seems plenty of surplus. I should have thought we could have let him have an extra fifty thousand. Is that what's worrying you?'

She smiled. Then pointed to the capital account.

He checked again, and looked up mystified. 'It balances. I agree there have been a lot of disposals. But that's up to Cazenoves. No doubt they're shifting the funds out of equities for some good reason.'

Silently she passed him two photocopies. The first was a letter to the stockbrokers, directing them to realize twenty-nine million pounds from equities to be held in a nominee account for the Trustees. The second was of a cheque, apparently sellotaped together from many small pieces, made out to Doge Investments for just over seven million pounds. It was, like all Ingram cheques, signed by Henry Ruggles on behalf of the Trustees, and drawn on the nominee account.

Tim raised his eyebrows. 'Doge Investments?' He picked up the *Financial Times* again and quickly scanned the commercial share listings. 'Who are they?'

She shrugged without replying. Tim leant back in his chair. Seven million pounds! No doubt Henry knew his business, and undoubtedly he had *carte blanche* to invest the funds, subject to a professional standard of care. Even so. He smiled at the silent young woman.

'Well,' he said, 'if anyone asks me, I can truthfully say you have said not a single word about this to me.' She nodded gratefully.

'You'd better return this,' he added, handing back the computer sheet. 'If you have copies of these,' he held up the other two documents, 'keep them at home. I'll hang on to them if I may.'

Without a word, she took the sheet, stood up and left. It was then that he suddenly remembered what had been bothering him. He hadn't thought about Flora all week. With a rueful grin, he settled back and returned to the crossword.

Chapter 22

Throughout August and into September the sun continued to bear down remorselessly. In a confused and angry state of mind, Max drove his long, open car north, accelerating through the sleepy market towns which lay astride roads almost empty of the traffic that, having clogged them for decades, now plunged like lemmings down the slip roads on to the stationary fume-laden motorways.

To hell with Amanda! To hell with Maria! To hell even with Perky! He never wanted to have to depend on another woman as long as he lived. He had an agreeably masculine cargo on board: thick shooting tweeds, an oily mackintosh coat, a rotting trilby, two shotguns swathed in dusters in their olive green velvet-lined leather cases, and a thousand cartridges distributed between two bags and a magazine. His spaniel sat cheerfully on the passenger seat beside him, tongue lolling, eyes alert. The worries of unpaid accounts and an overdraft made worse by his monthly cheque being unaccountably delayed evaporated in the dust from his tyres as he veered off the main road again at Piercebridge and started the long switchback route across the borders en route for Strathdhui.

When Lord Woodchester had idly invited him north at the party, he had thought no more of it. Then, following a further firm invitation by post, he had suddenly decided to cut loose and indulge a whim for revisiting Scotland, tasting again the refreshing bite of the cooler northern air and the exhilaration of the mountain scenery. It was thirty years since he had been to Strathdhui, a bleak granite shooting lodge sitting on the edge of a wide loch at the foot of Ben Skiech. In those days it had belonged to the Fitzwilliams, only recently supplanted by Lord Woodchester's lavish use of the millions he had made from electronics and heavy engineering.

Much of the road had changed. He could skirt Edinburgh now instead of clattering over its cobbles, and the Forth Road Bridge sent him soaring over the glistening water he had last crossed on a steam ferry. By teatime he was climbing the steep hill of the Lecht and could see the welcome patches of obstinate white snow on the Cairngorms. He stopped for a moment to allow his dog some relief. The spaniel plunged straight into the heather, disturbing a small covey of grouse who exploded out of their cover, flying low over the hillside with mocking cries.

'Come here, boy,' shouted Max. 'Come here, you fool!'

But he found himself smiling for the first time in weeks. Two tall granite pillars on the roadside surmounted by newly gilded leopards announced the Woodchester influence. Beyond them, a metalled road wound along the hillside past a ruined bothy and into a thick pinewood. On either side, tall foxgloves rose above the shaded bracken, lit here and there by shafts of brilliant sunlight penetrating the dense canopy of the trees. There was a sharp tang in the forest air and once, when he slowed for a pothole, he caught a glimpse of a roebuck, staring out anxiously through the greenish shadows. Then the trees began to recede, and the whole car juddered as he braked too late and clattered over a cattle grid flanked by a new deer fence decorated with a grisly line of dead vermin. Beyond the wood, the hillside opened out on either side and there below him stretched the dark-blue waters of Loch Dhui with the white-harled façade of the shooting lodge on its farther shore.

'My dear fellow!' Lord Woodchester cried as Max pulled up beneath the porch. 'Let me.' He seized Max's suitcase and cartridge bags.

'What a lovely spot,' said Max tactfully, suspecting that his host, like most of the newly established, would not wish to hear of his predecessors' reign.

'I must show you round!' said his delighted friend. 'Perhaps tomorrow after the shoot? The forecast is excellent.'

But Nature, impervious to forecasters and proud proprietors alike, decreed otherwise. That night a storm of biblical proportions embraced these islands, and Lord Woodchester's guests, abruptly deprived of electricity, huddled together for company in front of the spitting hall fire as the mountains around them vibrated with the shock of the thunder, and the tiny burns swelled into foaming cataracts stained brown with the peat.

'I'm very much afraid,' said Lord Woodchester over a chilly breakfast, peering through the streaming window at the driving rain, 'that it's going to be a day for bridge and billiards.'

'But it's the Ghillies Ball tonight!' cried his wife anxiously. 'Whenever will the Hydro Board reconnect us?'

'Riddell has gone to Aberdeen to fetch a generator,' replied her imperturbable husband. 'You will have power by this evening.'

'Can you really get one so soon?' asked Dapper, who had arrived the day before Max.

'Well, I certainly hope so,' replied his host, 'seeing that I own the company that makes them.'

In fact the first guests had begun to arrive that evening, each new group swept into the hall by gusts of wind and rain, before the lights of the house miraculously burst into life. Candles flickered everywhere and the subtle stench of oil lamps and paraffin stoves added to the enjoyable air of a crisis stoically overcome. Four pipers, one already almost too drunk to play, were seated in the gallery above the guests, and Lord Woodchester was dispensing small glasses of fiery whisky to all comers.

'Now then, Anderson!' he said to one plump old man wearing a red kilt under a motheaten green jacket secured by silver buttons. 'Who's that pretty gal you're with, eh?'

'My daughter, my lord,' replied the other.

'Don't think I've seen her out on the hill?'

The other drained his glass. 'No, my lord. She's been working as a secretary in London.'

'Here. Let me fill you up. Now,' Lord Woodchester raised his glass in the direction of Flora who was mutinously standing beside her mother, still protesting in an undertone at being dragged away from her book to pay obeisance to the local magnate, 'here's to hoping we see more of her up here. She's a real beauty.'

'Thank you, your Lordship,' said her father, who

had, after all, supplied the drink for the evening at an inflated profit. 'Perhaps you'll choose her to open the reels?'

Nor were theirs the only eyes on Flora. Dapper and Max, finding unexpected common cause in their shared dislike of the Ruggles family, were watching her from beside the chimneypiece.

'That's an uncommonly pretty girl,' said Max, drawing speculatively on his cigarette.

Dapper nodded. 'I've seen her before,' he said, 'but I can't think where.'

'Well, while you're thinking about it,' said his companion, 'I'm going to ask her to dance.' Chucking his cigarette into the fire, he marched over and put out his hand.

'May I introduce myself?' he said. 'I'm Max Ingram and I was hoping you might allow me to partner you in the first reel?'

Flora glared up at him, slightly alarmed by his superficial resemblance to the Colonel. But she took his hand, which was warm and leathery.

'I'm Flora Knox,' she said, deliberately emphasizing her accent as a veil of protection against a type that was all too familiar to her. 'My father keeps the Waddington Arms in Tomintoul.'

'Excellent!' laughed Max. 'Now we'll know where to go if the booze runs out.' He smiled at her.

There was a sudden scuffle. One of the pipers had slid off his chair and was slumped on the landing with one stockinged leg sticking out through the balustrade of the gallery. The others, after a brief struggle to try to extricate him, shouldered their instruments and, with a preliminary wail, launched into the reassuringly familiar skirl of the local reel, The Bride of Towie.

'Come on,' said Max, taking off his smoking jacket and laying it across a chair. 'Let's show these people how a reel should be danced.'

When Mr Anderson drove his family home in the early hours, his elderly Austin of England shooting brake weaving a serpentine course as the road swam in and out of focus, Flora sat beside him with an abstracted air. Her mother lay fast asleep across the back bench, cradled in her brother's arms. Flora was trying to remember Tim's face. Having spent two months hopelessly trying to forget it, she was unreasonably disturbed by discovering suddenly that she could no longer reliably call it to mind.

Chapter 23

The storm had laid waste the whole of Britain. In Newcastle, two suburbs were evacuated, in Cornwall a whole village was lost, and in Hampshire, Gervase Yeatley-Smith's canals first filled with water and then caved in, as the dehydrated soil, sapped by a myriad new streams, collapsed beneath the weight of the new foundations, scattering the freshly stone-clad walls into heaps of picturesque rubble.

'Good God!' shouted Captain Legge, when his telescope revealed the full extent of the disaster. 'Divine intervention! I'll never be rude to that bloody vicar again.' He could hardly bear to tear himself away to return to his breakfast.

'I just don't believe this.' After Gervase Yeatley-Smith's first panic-stricken call, Henry Ruggles had driven recklessly through the continuing storms to see for himself the havoc of the previous night.

The motorway had been comprehensively blocked by fallen pylons, but he had navigated his way through unexpected fords and little villages like Odiham where the main street was under three inches of brackish water, until, breasting the familiar rise, he looked down on a scene of romantic desolation. One façade of the new church remained, though half of the pillars of its triumphal portico had fallen, leaving the exuberant pediments balancing precariously in mid-air. Even through the driving rain, there was an undeniable beauty about the waterlogged canals, with their isolated chimneys and archways rising among heaps of white stone.

'Ecco il leone!'

Henry and the architect turned to face a round little man, wrapped in waterproofs, whose silver moustache jutted aggressively beneath a mottled blue nose.

'It's a quotation,' said the little man helpfully. 'From *Otello*.'

'You're trespassing, Captain Legge,' snapped Yeatley-Smith, 'as well you know. Kindly get off our land.'

'Your land?' The erstwhile scourge of the German navy bowed low. 'I beg your pardon, my dear sir. And is this our local Doge? Or do I mean Ozymandias, King of Kings?'

'Jim!' shouted the architect to his foreman who was standing, hands on hips, a few yards apart arguing with two journalists. 'Have Captain Legge escorted off the site, will you, there's a good fellow?'

The foreman, eagerly followed by his attendants, walked over with a grim expression. The little Captain held up his hands in a gesture of pacification.

'Don't worry, young man, I'm leaving. I just wanted to savour the sight of Venice in Peril. Only this time,' he said over his shoulder, 'I reckon it'll take a mite more saving.' Chuckling to himself, he waddled away through the mud.

'There's always one,' said Jim soothingly.

'What happens now?' asked Henry when he and the architect were again alone.

'Well,' sighed Yeatley-Smith. 'We'll have to clear the site and start again.

'*Start again*?' Henry's voice came out as a squeak.

'Just *look* at it,' said his exasperated companion. 'There's a year's work just in clearing up.'

Henry opened his mouth and stayed very still, as a violent wave of nausea shook his stocky frame.

'Yes,' continued the architect. 'It'll take seven months to get back to the starting point. Almost all the footings are affected and the drains have gone completely. The worst worry is the structures that remain. Some are decidedly unsafe and we'll have to wait for continuous frost before I can bring in machinery heavy enough to tackle the church. Although,' he mused, 'perhaps it would be cheaper to dynamite it and re-carve the front feature from scratch.'

The roaring in Henry's ears had risen to a crescendo, and overcome by this internal hurricane, he sank to his knees as the architect was speaking, dipping his steaming face thankfully into the chalky pool in which he had been standing.

'What are you doing now?' shouted the architect against the wind, noticing for the first time that his employer was not listening.

Henry's body, suddenly diminished in size, seemed to compress itself before flopping slowly over as the rainwater darkened the cloth of his suit with a sinister spreading stain.

'So you see,' said Robin grimly to Tim a week later, 'with my father dead, I wish to terminate the partnership. I don't like you, and I don't like working with you, and no doubt the feeling is mutual.' Both men were wearing black ties.

Tim shrugged. He had been expecting this. 'And the terms?'

'Oh,' Robin waved an airy hand, 'no doubt Willows Jardine will handle all that. It was all carefully provided for in the original partnership deed. That's how they got rid of Cavendish so easily. Now it's your turn. I don't think you and I need trouble ourselves. But I should like it to be from today. I have prepared a memorandum.' He slipped a sheet of paper over the desk.

Tim read it through twice. 'This restrains me from communicating with any of our existing clients,' he said.

'Oh quite,' said Robin, wiping his lips. 'Since you own only a minority third of the business, I think that's to be expected, don't you? You can't expect to be paid for the goodwill element of our business if you want to walk away with the clients as well. But I'll make an exception if you like.' He smiled wolfishly. 'You can keep the Gumby business.'

Tim laughed. 'I'll sign this if I get a full indemnity against any retrospective claims on the partnership and if my share of the business is agreed to be valued as of today, and paid within fourteen days, as a fundamental condition, with interest payable thereafter at our Client Rate.'

Robin narrowed his eyes. 'That's a lot of money you're talking about,' he said.

Tim shrugged again. 'Those are my terms. I passed George Willows sheltering at the tube station so I know he's in. I'll sign all three documents together,' he looked at his wristwatch, 'when I get back here at four this afternoon.'

'Done.' Robin gathered up his papers and left the room. Immediately the telephone rang.

'Yes?'

'Is that Tim Bryce?' A soft and friendly voice.

'Yes.'

'This is Laura Ingram. I wondered how my little idea stood.' She felt she had no choice but to be persistent.

'Well,' replied Tim. 'It's a little awkward.'

'Oh?' She swallowed hard. Was he going to refuse to deal with her?

'You may not have heard that Henry Ruggles, the Senior Partner, has just died.'

There was a silence.

'Oh dear,' she said, trying not to appear relieved. 'He was such a kind old man. I'm so sorry.'

'And I'm actually leaving the partnership today,' he added.

'Oh?' She sounded incredulous, and then resigned. 'Yes. I see.'

'So, really, you should speak to Robin Ruggles.'

'No,' she said. 'I want to deal with you.' She was suddenly very positive, unexpectedly firm.

'But . . .'

'We can meet next week when you've sorted it all out. I shall expect you to call me, but if you don't, I shall call you.' And rang off.

Tim lunched at his club, and when he returned to High Holborn, he found Robin with George Willows, their neighbouring solicitor who was brought in from time to time when independent advice was needed, putting the final touches to a ten-page document. Robin paid no attention to Tim's question about Laura.

'Talk to the little tart as much as you like,' he said, 'but don't touch the Ingram Trust business if you want to keep your money.'

'This is all highly irregular,' grumbled Willows, peering at Tim through his thick bifocals. 'But your accountants say it'll only take them a week to settle the valuation, as the business was being valued for probate anyway. Trust a lawyer to complicate things.'

No-one laughed.

'You're content to act for both sides?' asked Tim cautiously.

'Oh yes,' said the other. 'I don't see a conflict. It's all straightforward as the goodwill element is specified and that only leaves the value of your lease here. Your pension is fully portable. The rest is up to the accountants. It's just the rush.'

Tim gestured at his former partner who was feeling in his pocket for a pen.

'Here we go,' said Robin, and started signing. Tim followed suit with one of the clerks witnessing both sets.

'I'll get these copied,' the clerk said and hurried out of the room.

'Well,' said Tim.

But Robin walked over to the window. 'Get out!' he said without turning round.

'I have to collect my private papers,' replied Tim, more contemptuous than hurt, 'and I have some goodbyes to say to old friends.'

'Oh, no doubt,' sneered the other. 'But I want you out within the hour. This is my territory from now on.'

Tim began to gather his few personal possessions and pack them into his briefcase. After a bit, he left the room, closing the door quietly behind him.

Tim did think a couple of times about ringing Laura Ingram, but since he was contracted not to involve himself in her business affairs, what was the point? But Laura's new-found determination did not desert her. The following Friday he came home in the evening to find three messages on his ansaphone.

'Mr Bryce? Hello, Mr Bryce? Are you there? This is Brian the plumber. I've checked that downpipe, and I've been looking round in the workshop to try . . .' Tim pressed the fast-forward button.

'Darling! It's me-ee! Are you in the little girl's room? Come *on*, you slag! Pick the fucking phone up!' He groaned with impatience. Wrong numbers were getting more, not less, frequent. And then a cool clipped voice, 'Tim? This is Laura Ingram. I'll keep trying, but ring me back if you get this before we speak.' As he noted down her name on the red leather pad, the telephone began to ring.

'Yes?'

It was her. 'Tim?'

'Hello.' What on earth was there to say to her?

'Can we meet for a drink at Oriel's? I want to ask you a couple of questions.'

He had nothing else to do. 'Why not?'

'Six-thirty?'

He looked at his watch. It was nearly six. He would walk there. 'Fine.'

'See you!' She rang off. Rather reluctantly, he climbed the stairs to his bedroom, its high ceiling decorated with deep carvings of fruit executed in a dark grainy wood, and pulled off his clothes. He crossed the corridor to his father's old dressing room, in search of the thick red poloneck he kept for autumn walks. Something bright in the corner of the room caught his eye. It was almost hidden behind the legs of the heavy bureau. Stooping, he found it was a skimpy cotton blouse. Flora's. Why on earth had he never spotted it before? With a wry smile, he stuffed it into the wastepaper basket. Let Mrs Nico, the cleaner, make whatever she wanted out of that. It showed how seldom she came into this room!

Turning down the King's Road, he inhaled the chilly autumn air, great gulps of blissful reminiscence. He had passed these very shops in his pushchair, and on the way to school. Who wanted the countryside when they could observe the rich variety of a city street? A woman walking towards him suddenly smiled at him. But her face was wholly unfamiliar. He began to panic, and then realized, to his surprise, that he himself was already smiling, in fact laughing at the ludicrous memories of youth. Laura was sitting at a window table when he arrived.

'That's funny,' she said. 'I've never seen you in anything but a suit before.'

He grinned and looked down at his faded green jeans. 'I know. It's quite a change, not having a job.'

'What will you do?' She had a glass of red wine in front of her. 'Like one of these?'

He shook his head. 'Do you have fresh orange juice?' The surly young waiter, who had rather reluctantly responded to Laura's raised hand, nodded and wandered away towards the other tables. 'I'm having a month or so off, just sitting back and looking around.'

'A gentleman of leisure.' As soon as she'd said it, she deeply regretted the words. His carefree expression, which had lifted her spirits, vanished, making way for a guarded scowl. Was it just with her that he was so touchy?

'What was it you wanted to see me about?' He was itching to go home, to get away from someone who seemed intent on offending him. With Robin's cheque for nearly four million pounds sitting in his deposit account, he had no taste for the gibes of masterful young women, however glamorous. She leant over the table and took his hand.

'Don't be offended,' she said. 'You're very touchy with me.' He stared at her. 'I'm sure it's my fault,' she continued, still resting her hand on his. It was very light, like the hand of a child. 'I do understand that you can't handle anything to do with the dreaded Trust, but I don't want to lose touch, and I wondered if you'd come to *Traviata* with me at Covent Garden next Tuesday. They've got Stephanita and Rankin singing.'

'I'd love to!' he said, and suddenly remembered his earlier invitation to her. So what? Hers was a generous suggestion, and he was grateful. 'Thank you very much.' He looked at her, and for the first time he registered her as a woman, rather than as a client or an adversary. Filtered through the gauze of seven years of alienation, his mind unconventionally focused less on her appearance than on the strength of character and good-natured serenity which he felt projected into his circumspect awareness.

'Was yours the coffee?' The waiter was back, and evidently in no mood for contradiction since he placed the cup firmly beside Tim and departed.

'So what will you do now?'

Tim shrugged. 'I really don't know.'

'I can imagine. Can I really not escape from your old firm? I simply loathe Robin. And I trust you.'

Tim grinned, remembering his erstwhile partner's ambitions as this woman's husband. 'Not easily,' he admitted. 'You could try talking to General Morne. He is your sole Trustee until another one is appointed to act with him. But it's highly likely he'll appoint Robin, and then you will be stuck with him.'

'What's the General like?'

'I don't know,' said Tim. 'I've never met him.'

At a loss for further conversation, she looked at her wristwatch. Abruptly she stood up and placed some coins on the table. 'This has been fun,' she said. 'Now don't forget. Next Tuesday. Seven-thirty it starts. I'll be waiting for you in the foyer.' With a swift movement, she bent down and brushed his cheek with her lips. After she had left, he stayed at the table for some time, staring after her.

Chapter 24

It was several weeks before the full extent of Tim's financial good fortune became apparent. It started that weekend with a single paragraph in the *Independent*, recounting the precipitate failure of the well-known architecture practice Yeatley-Smith Associates and bewailing the continuing trend of collapse in the building sector. Like many businesses, Yeatley-Smith had been operating with a substantial overdraft secured against the good name of the partnership, and the profits of current and anticipated future business. Once it became apparent that his major contract was going to yield nothing except a hailstorm of writs from equally embattled sub-contractors and that his own insurers were querying whether his work in specifying and overseeing the foundations had met professional guidelines, it was just a matter of hours before his bank foreclosed, though not before two groups of enraged contractors had stormed the site and looted substantial quantities of building materials to offset against their own losses.

When Laura saw Tim's head bobbing above the crowd in the opera house, the first thing she said was, 'I saw my Aunt Gwen today. She says she hasn't had her monthly cheque, and could you please go back and sort Robin out!'

'You're looking very lovely,' he said, gradually

taking in the black silk jersey number and the jet choker.

'Look! There's old Lady Woodchester with her walker,' she cried to distract his attention from her boiling blush. She had tried on seven outfits before settling on this one, and wasn't having the effect of his first compliment spoiled by a crimson complexion. 'And there's poor Maria, my father's ex,' she added in an undertone as a tall woman with large mournful eyes crossed the landing above them, her arm firmly supporting an elderly man walking with two sticks.

'I didn't know he'd been married before,' said Tim.

'Mistress, silly, not wife. That's her husband. He's a composer or something.'

'Ah.'

'Here's your programme. I've ordered some Chablis and smoked salmon sandwiches for the interval. That suit?' He was slightly at a loss.

After the performance, she led him down the street, and then down some stairs into a long low restaurant filled with the babble of thirty animated tables of cheerful diners.

'Have you ordered here too?' he asked, amused.

'I certainly have. We've got arugula and parmesan salad, followed by scallops in ginger with green beans in oil and lemon. If you're very good, I may let you choose the pudding.'

He stared at her across the table. 'Are you always so masterful?' To his surprise, he rather liked it.

'I'm going to admit something to you,' she said, 'but not until Giovanni's brought me some reviving Orvieto. Here it comes.' She grabbed her glass and drank deeply. 'Now! Don't look so alarmed.' He was in a state of some tension. 'I made a dreadful mistake when you asked me out many years ago. I'd like to think you've forgotten, but as you probably haven't, I want to say sorry.' He raised his hands in a confused mime of defence. 'I'm sure it makes it impossible for you to look on me as anything except a spoilt brat, but I really like being with you, and more than anything, I trust your judgement.' He was quite unable to reply. 'Now let's eat, and then I want you to teach me a bit about the Law of Trusts. There's no such thing as a free night out, and I'm determined to learn how to sort out my Trust and get rid of bloody Robin Ruggles at the same time. You're on for Tristan next week?' He nodded dumbly. It was easier to concentrate on the arugula than face her burning eyes.

While Tim and Laura continued to meet regularly to discuss tactics for extracting her money from Robin's grasp, more ripples of unease started to emanate from members of the Ingram family as their monthly payments suddenly ceased, accompanied by fulsome letters from Robin explaining that with his father's decease, the administration of the Trust had to be routed via Northern Ireland pending the appointment of a new trustee.

Telephone calls to Morne Abbey were met with the discouraging news that General Morne was bedridden (as had been the case for several years) and was thus unable to speak to anyone, the Abbey telephone system never having penetrated beyond its original position in the basement kitchen corridor.

Then came a thunderbolt. '*Dear Miss Ingram,*' ran Laura's copy of a general family missive from Drax, Pelham and Trent, the accountants. '*As auditors to the Estate of your late grandfather, Major Tollemache Ingram, we regret to have to inform you that serious irregularities have appeared in the Trust accounts.*

Recent very heavy investments were made in a property company set up by the late Mr Henry Ruggles. Not only was a substantial body of the Trust funds transferred to this property company named Doge Investments, but it also took out a very considerable loan from a major American bank secured on the remaining corpus of the Trust. In so far as I have been able to communicate with General Morne, it appears that he was not fully aware of this unusual course of action, but since he signed all the relevant documentation, there is a prima facie case that repayment of this loan may be successfully sought from the Estate by the bank concerned.

'*The business of the property company was highly speculative and there seems little prospect of its remaining assets being of more than nominal value when set against its liabilities. The position is so serious that all payments from the Estate of your grandfather will have to be suspended for the foreseeable future. All properties owned by the Estate, such as your apartment, must be considered to be at risk.*'

Having read this letter, Laura sat back in her chair and stared at the photograph of her parents in its serpentine silver frame. What on earth would they do if Milston had to be sold? Her father had mysteriously stayed on in Scotland, sending occasional postcards from an address in Grantown on Spey where he had apparently taken a cottage for some fishing after leaving the Woodchesters. Her mother had just shrugged – she was past caring about her husband's semi-detached truancy.

Blissfully unaware of the change in his fortunes, Max

sat by the river bank, his throat wrapped in a thick scarf against the autumn chill. Beside him, Flora was busy unpacking their lunch, some baps filled with bacon, a couple of hardboiled eggs wrapped in silverfoil, and two bottles of McEwan's Export ale.

'I love you,' he said for the umpteenth time that day, waiting anxiously for her reassuring echo.

'Now do tell,' he said, casting his fly far across the water to bob temptingly back over the surface of a dark little pool, 'was Charles Chesterfield really such a monster?'

Flora had courageously decided to confide in her new lover, who had courted her for a month with a delicacy that would have astounded his family, and which caused no less unease in the Waddington Arms.

'He's older than I am,' protested her father, when Max's visits became too frequent to be ignored.

'Well, Father,' replied Flora, 'so was Mr Knox.'

'Ah, but is he married?' was her mother's quiet contribution from beside the hearth in the family quarters at the back of the inn. Flora made no reply, not knowing the answer. After that, there was much wagging of heads behind her back until an elaborate set of discreet enquiries via the servants at Strathdhui Lodge brought the disquieting news that the dark Englishman was indeed a married man.

Watching Max's skilful work with the rod, Flora pursed her lips. 'No,' she said. 'I'd no call him exactly a monster. He liked his own way, but which man doesn't?'

Max chuckled. 'No wonder he was looking so out of sorts at Goodwood. But his bad luck,' he turned towards her and smiled, softening the aggressive cast of his face, 'is my great good luck.' On an impulse, he had laid down his rod, and made to gather her to him. She placed her hand on his chest.

'Max,' she said, 'I have to know. Is it true you're married?'

Instantly his smile vanished, his face dark again, even savage. 'You've never asked me that, not once,' he said.

'No,' she said simply. 'It doesn't matter to me. But my parents have been at me. And I'd rather know from you.'

He picked up his rod again, and sent the line whistling back over his head before hurling it far upstream.

'I am married,' he said grimly. 'But not in so happy a state as your parents. My wife lives in Dorset.'

'And you?' She was interested.

'I? Yes, well, sometimes in Dorset, but we have a house in Chester Square and I spend most of my time there.'

'Well,' she said, munching on an egg, 'thank you.'

'For what?' He had his back to her.

'For answering my question.' She moved up against him, so that her arms met round his waist, 'I do love you, you know.'

He grunted. The fly came floating past.

'Are there no damned fish in this blasted river?' he demanded.

'You might do better with a worm,' she murmured.

'Well, if there are no fish . . .' He was smiling now and anticipating his intentions, Flora began to unbutton her skirt.

When he got back to his cottage that night,

there were two letters waiting for him. One was the auditor's report, forwarded from Milston, the other was a polite letter from his bank, seeking an early meeting to discuss a timetable for reducing his overdraft.

Chapter 25

Robin's first reaction to his father's sudden death had been one of simple mourning. The old man had been kind and generous to him. He had loved his son despite (or perhaps because of) his obvious failings, and if he had been disappointed, he had never shown it. As the only child, Robin had inherited his father's share of the business, the suburban villa, a holiday penthouse in Eastbourne, and over a million pounds invested in middle-range British and American securities. There would be tax to pay, of course, but he was already a rich man through his own interest in the partnership. He knew he could afford now to feel agreeably secure, despite the very substantial loan, nearly three million pounds, he had had to negotiate to pay off Tim's share.

Then came the strange news about Doge Investments. At first it seemed no more than that — a rather wilful exchange of Trust investments. Only when the full enormity of what his father had done, without the slightest rational hint of explanation, became clear did Robin's feelings towards him begin to change. The loan to the ill-fated property company from an American bank was for eighteen million pounds, and the whole of the joint proceeds, amounting to over forty-five million pounds, had been paid over to the building contractors via the now bankrupt Yeatley-Smith Associates. True, there were eight hundred acres of land with building consent in prime Hampshire, but against that had to be set the rehabilitation costs of removing the colossal wreckage, together with the legal costs likely to arise from the contractors, several of whom were already in receivership. It was a total disaster. It was also a total mystery.

Among his father's papers he found a mass of architectural drawings, some by Yeatley-Smith, but some also in his father's hand, apparently going back many years – scribbles on the back of old letters, vast and elaborate fantasies, showing a love of architecture and a grasp of its intricacies that Henry Ruggles had never, even remotely, hinted at to his son. How could his father have left him such a poisoned legacy?

The outcry from the Ingram family had swollen to the point that he was obliged to call a meeting. The conference room at High Holborn was packed with more members of the clan than perhaps had ever come together before. Max had come down from Scotland and sat at the front between Laura and his sister Gwen. Across the room, in his motorized wheelchair, the eldest brother, Edgar, was surrounded by his six grown-up children, one of whom had brought her teenage daughters to learn their fate. The middle brother, Thady, a bachelor with a thick grey beard, who was something in the book trade, could be heard arguing noisily with General Morne's factotum. The latter, a stout balding man in a shiny blue suit, had come (under protest) to represent the sole surviving Trustee. Behind Max, also supported by her children, sat his widowed sister Deirdre, a sour-faced woman with thick pebble lenses, clearly in no mood to trifle with whoever was responsible for her imminent destitution.

'Ladies and Gentlemen!' Robin, flanked by George Willows and Drax, the man from the auditors, raised his voice to quell the hum of discontent. Willows was there for no reason other than to act for Robin in the event of threats of litigation against the firm or his father's estate. What with wives, ex-wives and one or two personal advisers, Robin was facing more than thirty hostile faces.

'Let me begin by giving you the facts.'

'As you see them,' muttered Thady loud enough to reassure his relations that the battle would be hard fought.

Ignoring the interruption, Robin began to read from a prepared statement: 'The Trustees . . .'

'You mean your father!'

Max stood up. 'I think,' he said, 'that we had better let Mr Ruggles read his speech so that we can consider it.' Edgar nodded vigorously, and silence fell again. Max sat down.

'I repeat,' said Robin 'the Trustees set up a company, in the name of Doge Investments, which was apparently intended to take advantage of the housing market . . .'

'What sodding housing market?' This in a high cracked voice from Deirdre.

'I repeat, to take advantage of the housing market, to build very prestigious commuter houses in Hampshire. This end of the market remains firm, and the acquisition of the land, and awarding of the construction contracts, were all made under very favourable terms. Unfortunately the September storm severely damaged the development, with the result that a scheme intended greatly to enhance the value of the Estate, and thus the payments made to the beneficiaries of Major Tollemache Ingram's Will, has instead resulted in substantial temporary loss. While it is hoped that some return will eventually accrue to you all from this venture, there is a short-term problem in that the additional capital needed to finance the scheme came in the form of a second loan from the Fifth Wisconsin Bank Corporation. And they are demanding immediate repayment.'

'How much?' Edgar, despite being nearly eighty, had a deep strong growl of a voice.

'Er.' Robin looked down at Drax. The accountant continued to stare towards the back of the room as if entirely divorced from the main action. Robin then consulted a second piece of paper.

'With interest,' he read, 'the current total amounts in all to nineteen million three hundred and seventeen thousand pounds, or thereabouts.'

'*Or thereabouts*! NINETEEN MILLION pounds!' Thady's voice had risen to a shriek to match his sister's. 'How much did all this tomfoolery cost, in God's name?'

'The total investment,' read Robin, who was beginning to pray for another tempest to destroy the building and all those within it, 'was forty-six million seven hundred and eleven thousand pounds, not counting one invoice outstanding which we are disputing with the architect's receivers.'

An absolute hush descended on the room. Even in their wildest dreams, this family could not have anticipated a calamity so complete.

'Of course he was mad,' said Gwen. 'Stark staring mad.'

'Just remind me,' cut in Edgar, 'of the current

disposition of the Trust funds, if you would, Mr Ruggles?'

Robin bowed. This time Drax did respond, and handed him a page of typewritten notes. 'After the money switched from the Trust's existing investments during the summer, there remain six million pounds split equally between quoted shares and medium-term gilts, together with just over two million on deposit against the Capital Gains Tax liability arising from the sale of securities,' he said. 'The remaining sixteen million pounds, at the nineteen eighty-eight valuation, is invested in property occupied by the beneficiaries.'

'And the current valuation of this calamitous property company?'

'I think, for practical purposes,' said Robin unhappily, 'that we have to treat that as being neutral.'

'Neutral,' repeated Edgar, savouring the word. 'Neutral. That is your way of saying that your father poured forty-seven million pounds of our money down a very large drain?' A disconcerting noise came from the inner workings of his chair, a sort of independent humming screech.

'The Trustees,' murmured Robin. 'The Trustees.'

'Your father, sir!' thundered Edgar, threshing about in his wheelchair in a sudden paroxysm of rage. 'An unmitigated scoundrel! You should be ashamed to bear his name.' Robin flushed angrily and opened his mouth.

'Hear me out!' bellowed the old man. 'If we accept your explanation – and I for one do not,' there were rumbles of agreement round the room, 'the corollary is that a further twelve million has to be raised from property valued at the height of the property boom at no more than sixteen million! In short, he has ruined us all.'

'I'd like to say something.' Laura's voice was very calm and cool set against her uncle's fury.

'Please,' said Robin. Sweat was pouring out of his hair and dripping off his ears and nose.

'I think there are two points to be considered,' Laura said. 'The first is whether the Trustees were acting legally in making these astonishing decisions. And if they were, the second is whether the bank was justified in making such a large advance without enquiring more closely into the legal position. I should like to hear from General Morne's agent who I believe is with us.' She turned and smiled courteously at the little round man who was busy cleaning out his ear behind her.

'Well, certainly,' said Robin after casting an anxious glance at Willows. 'Mr – er – Goulding?'

Mr Goulding stood up. 'The General is very sorry not to be here today,' he said, 'but as I expect you know, he keeps to his bed, the poor old fellow.'

'What I want to know,' said Laura, 'is to what extent he authorized this transaction?'

'Oh I can answer that,' butted in Robin, desperately. 'I have all the papers here, duly signed. There's no doubt about that.'

'I should like Mr Goulding's view, please,' said Laura. The poor man shifted uneasily from one foot to another. He raised his hand to explore his ear again and then halted it in mid-air, seemingly turned to stone.

'Mr Goulding?'

'Yes, Miss?'

'How much do you think the General knew of these transactions?'

The man shook his head. 'I really couldn't say, Miss.'

'He never discussed it with you?'

'Oh no, Miss.'

'Did you read the papers?'

'Well,' he shifted his feet again, 'not really, Miss. Only as much as was necessary.'

'And how much was that, exactly?'

There was some shuffling of other feet, as members of the family became impatient with this sideshow. So she smiled very warmly at him and he, feeling secure of her good opinion, added, 'Just so as I could show him where to sign.'

Suddenly he was the object of everyone's concentrated attention.

'You showed him where to sign?'

'Oh yes, Miss. You see,' with a burst of candour, 'the poor creature's been all but blind these past four years.'

It was only Laura's dramatic outstretching of her arm that prevented an explosion of outrage from her relatives.

'I know,' she said sympathetically. 'The poor man. But Mr Henry Ruggles knew, didn't he?'

'Oh yes,' replied Mr Goulding trustingly, above Robin's despairing shout. 'He said it didn't really matter.'

'I didn't know you were such an expert,' said Max admiringly after they had left the building, whence the sound of raised voices could be heard down in the street.

'I'm not,' said Laura demurely. 'Tim coached me.'

'Tim?' Max could never hear her mention a man's name without a spasm of involuntary jealousy.

'Tim Bryce. He's left the firm and I've asked him to handle my affairs.'

'I didn't know he'd left,' mused her father. 'He was the only sensible one there. How long have you known him?'

'Longer than you might think,' she said with a triumphant little smile. 'I've always admired him from afar.'

'Oh, indeed?'

'Yes,' she said. 'In fact, the only reason I used to see the unspeakable Robin Ruggles was in the hopes of his leading me to Tim. But,' she added, 'since we're talking of men and women, I want you to tell me what's so enticing about the north of Scotland in mid-October?'

Max looked at his watch. 'I've an appointment at Barclay's,' he said. 'Let's have dinner tonight. Come round to Chester Square.'

'Can I bring Tim?'

'If you must. Eight o'clock?'

'We'll be there.'

Chapter 26

'It could make quite a difference,' said Tim, examining the uneven burning of one of Max's cigars.

'But old Ruggles wasn't *that* rich, surely?' objected Max. They were sitting in the upstairs drawing room, a tall apartment with long french windows overlooking the peaceful square. 'I suppose we'll have to sell Milston. At least this house belongs to Amanda.' Laura shot him a quizzical look which silenced him abruptly.

'No,' said Tim thoughtfully. 'It's not that his estate can pay it off, though I banked a very substantial sum for my small share in the business.'

'Did you indeed?' said Max, with sudden interest. He had been worrying about Laura's prospects all day. 'Another glass of brandy?'

'No thank you.' Leaving the law firm had had a remarkable effect on Tim's consumption of alcohol. While far from teetotal, he had, without immediately noticing any change himself, altogether stopped drinking during the day while still enjoying whatever came his way during the evening. 'No – the point is,' Tim was pursuing his own line of thought, 'the partnership of course had professional indemnity through Lloyds against malpractice or incompetence. It's an unheard of sum, but I think a claim might just hold.'

'You mean they'll pay us back?' Max could scarcely believe what he was hearing.

'I think they might be prepared to make a good offer to avoid being sucked into litigation,' said Tim cautiously.

'We're talking about nearly fifty million pounds!'

'They won't like it, and you may have to fight for it, but, yes, in my judgement, there's a case now Laura has established that Henry Ruggles knew that his co-trustee couldn't function properly. Therefore he was committing professional misconduct, and on a princely scale.'

'I do hope you're right,' sighed Laura. 'I've been so worried about the Stubbses, and wondering what would happen to Bill and Maisie.'

'Poor old Lloyds,' muttered Max gloomily. 'Thady's a name, you know, and so is old Deirdre. No wonder they looked so glum! It's a miracle they can smile at all. But tell me more about your plans. Why did you quit the business?'

'Robin threw me out.'

'Luckiest day of your life, I should say.'

Tim nodded. 'I've had three good offers,' he said. 'I think I may join Linklaters. I've got exactly three clients to bring with me at the moment.'

'Laura . . .'

'Laura, Dapper Gumby and Perky Metternich.' Max's face was a study.

'Oh, that Perky!' said Laura bravely, stifling her jealousy. 'How often that woman pops up. I wouldn't have thought she was your type.'

'You know very well that she isn't,' said Tim with feeling. 'But I do rather like her. She's good fun and she rang me out of the blue last week to say she had had a row with Farrers, and would I take over? I haven't the faintest idea yet what it entails, if anything.'

'I should guess,' said Max heavily, 'that it entails quite a lot.'

'She was very much Daddy's type,' murmured Laura with a sly smile.

'Well, I'm off to bed,' said her sorely tried parent. 'I've got some telephoning to do.'

'Anyone we know?' asked Laura.

'No,' he said. 'Definitely not.'

After he had gone, Tim stayed on for half an hour. As he was leaving, he said, 'I'm giving Dapper lunch at The Savoy tomorrow to celebrate my taking on my first clients. Will you join us?'

'Only if Perky is coming too!' She was determined to conquer her weakness by the most direct means.

'Yes,' said Tim. 'That's a good idea, I'll see if she's free.'

The lunch was a great success. They drank champagne, Perky and Tim indirectly commiserating with Laura and Dapper for the strange reversal of their roles, whereby the latter pair, who had both been born to great inheritances, were, for the moment at least, reduced almost to penury, while the others, although neither of them admitted as much, were decidedly prosperous. After lunch, Perky announced that she was going to visit friends in Windsor.

'Can I cadge a lift off you?' said Dapper almost shyly.

'Of course,' she said. 'Where are you heading?'

'If you drop me at the Hogarth roundabout,' he said, 'I've got a friend in Chiswick who's putting me up at the moment. I'd like a walk by the river to clear my head after all Tim's hospitality.'

They walked off in companionable silence, leaving Tim to find a taxi for Laura before walking down to the Temple to deal with some unfinished business over his release.

'When shall I see you again?' she said out of the window as he turned to go.

'I'll ring,' he said, 'when I've explored the indemnity position. Tell your mother not to worry.'

He raised a hand and hurried away, anxious to conceal his complicated thoughts. Was he falling in love again? Was her unconcealed admiration for him an encouragement or a discouragement? At least he could truthfully claim to be indifferent to whether she was rich or poor. Three months ago he would have given every penny to have Flora back in his arms. Three months! He had expected to pass many dreary years regretting her loss. And yet here he was fizzing with desire for another woman, even contemplating — well, perhaps not. The shutter in his brain activated itself at the softest whisper of the idea of marriage.

The hours he had spent with her discussing the law, and then coaching her for the family meeting, had led not only to a deepening friendship, but also, more crucially, to considerable respect for her energetic and humorous character. The utter lack of complaint at being catapulted from great wealth to the real threat of being thrown out of her home impressed him all the more because it came not from rigorous self-restraint, but from a genuine absence of rancour. If anything, she seemed to welcome the challenge, her main concern being for her parents' dependants: the Stubbs, and Bob and Maisie Crawley in the lodge. What if whoever bought Milston did not keep them on?

Tim was not perhaps the first man to be surprised by his feelings for an ostensibly casual companion. One minute she was his avid pupil, another he was laughing at some gently sarcastic dig at his lawyer's precision, and more and more often he caught himself gazing at her body, and longing to take her in his arms. Nor was there any obvious sign that she would object!

Oh come *on*, you *fool*, he thought to himself. What's so wrong with marriage? The shutter was bulging but clinging on tight. He pounded one fist with the other, and that poor shutter flew open. 'Yes!' he said aloud. 'I could marry her.'

Suddenly he knew what he sought from marriage. It was neither sanctimonious giving nor self-absorbed taking. It was very simple after all: Laura beside him, sharing their lives. Astounded at his own mental freedom (and no less so than the man behind the paperstand listening avidly to this public soliloquy), he laughed out loud. He ran on down the cobbles and up three flights of stairs to the chambers where he was already overdue.

Perky, meanwhile, in leading Dapper to where she had parked her car on the Embankment, experienced that sinking feeling only too familiar to London motorists, of finding her compact Mercedes convertible the subject of professional interest. The clamper, a stocky man in striped overalls, was actually in the process of sliding his yellow contraption athwart her offside front wheel as she ran up.

'Oh please!' she said, panting with exhaustion, 'I really am so sorry!'

The man looked up ready with a stock retort, but Dapper saw, with the wry recognition of one man for another's susceptibility, the official's face change from truculence to a kind of softened respect. There was no doubt that Perky, without even meaning to, cast a very infectious enchantment over males. It was not simply her appearance, nor the grace of her movements, nor even the subtle comedy of her easy-going humour; it was perhaps more her aura of affectionate empathy, allied with a whiff of sexual danger. But emotional or physical, whatever it was was enough for this stranger to withdraw his instrument of torture, put it back in his truck, snarl at his astounded colleague and drive off, all accomplished without changing the idiotic smile on his face which turned constantly back for yet one last smile of thanks from the goddess.

'Very bad for you!' said Dapper with a grin as she swung the car out into the traffic.

'A kind man,' she replied.

'A besotted fool more like. They make a vast commission out of each victim.'

'You would have carried on clamping?' He laughed at her droll expression and nodded, and when she spun the wheel to turn past the Houses of Parliament, flinging his body against hers, he felt a surge of desire for this unattainable animal beside him. What a waste – the thousands of acres, the lorryloads of old paintings, the rows of cottages in Gumby-St-Leonard's, all sold for such empty extravagance when they could have been devoted to a woman whose key was the simplest of them all: hard cash!

'What are you laughing at?' she asked, as they sped past the ruinous council tenements of Pimlico, enjoying the chill of the autumn with its sharp scent of decay.

'I honestly don't know,' he said ruefully. 'There isn't that much to laugh at. But I do enjoy your company. Tim is a good friend, isn't he? I think we're both in safe hands there.' She didn't reply, concentrating on turning right against the clear instructions of a road sign to avoid the sudden congestion by Chelsea Bridge.

'Tell me what happened with your court case,' she said, and he was still making her laugh when they reached the Hogarth roundabout.

'Here we are then!'

'Here we are.' Accustomed to masking his feelings, Dapper let himself out of the car without delay. 'Thanks for the lift.'

'Not a bit.'

'Goodbye.'

'Goodbye.'

He walked away down the pavement, his head full of accelerating hopeless thoughts, the sort of thoughts entirely alien to his usual insouciance. For no particular reason, believing her to be already far away among the droning traffic, he turned round. She was still there, too distant to make out her expression, but watching him.

Who can explain why two people, who have lived their lives so exclusively for themselves, egotists to the extreme, should suddenly fall in love? The stern analysts of the human condition (the cynics and those to whom the truth must be ruthlessly isolated by peeling away the valueless and misleading pith of emotion) tell us that 'romantic love' is a myth, bright Christmas paper designed to conceal the reality: three parts fantasy to one part calculated need. And yet, how much is hidden from them, these self-denying apostles of flat earthism, who can neither see nor imagine anything beyond their own arid materialism!

Dapper stood there for a few moments longer, accustoming himself to his new mood. Then with the slightest of waves, really just a flicker of one gloved hand, she had gone. With a smile, he continued on his way north through the suburbs.

By seven o'clock that night, Tim was outside Laura's apartment, his finger stabbing impatiently at her bell.

'Who is it?'

'Tim.'

'Come on up. First floor on the right.'

'No!' he said. 'Come down. I want to show you my home.'

There was a pause. 'All right,' she said. 'I'll be down in five minutes.'

He packed her into his taxi and they drove in silence to Chelsea.

'Here we are,' he said.

'My!' she murmured. 'It's rather large.'

'But cosy,' he said, paying off the smiling driver.

He showed her the whole house, from the old-fashioned kitchen in the basement to his father's studio in the attic with the garish studies in oils stacked against the wall. Then they went down to the library where he lit a fire.

Standing up, he said, 'Will you marry me?'

Laura stared at him, a strong flush mounting from her breasts until her face was suffused with a crimson glow.

'Well?' he said again, horribly uncertain whether she was angry or pleased. He had schooled himself to expect another rejection, and to accept it equably, however she might deliver it. But he trusted her, believing now in her generosity of spirit where before he had doubted. Time seemed suspended – he became ridiculously conscious of the motion of the clock's pendulum, of the shadow on his father's self-portrait, of . . .

'Yes,' she said. 'Yes.' As he moved to kiss her, the telephone rang with shrill insistence. He picked up the receiver.

'Tim? Tim?'

'Yes,' he said, alarmed by the frantic voice. 'Who is it?'

'It's me, Perky. I need legal advice. You've got to come now. Please come!' He could hear sobbing.

'What's the matter? Tell me what's the matter.'

Laura put her arm round his shoulder. 'What is it?' she whispered.

'He raped me,' Perky was saying in his other ear. 'Colonel Chesterfield raped me. The police are here now.'

Chapter 27

'You mean he actually raped you?' Tim was sitting beside Perky on her sofa, drinking the strong black coffee she had forced herself to down.

'Yes.'

'And you told the police?'

'Yes. Was that wrong?'

'No!' said Tim robustly. 'Of course not. But you'll have to prepare yourself for quite an ordeal.'

'It can't be worse than what happened,' she muttered, her teeth chattering with delayed shock.

'Knowing the Colonel, he's hardly likely to plead guilty.'

She stared at him. 'You mean?'

'I mean there'll be a trial? And they'll try to say you led him on.'

'Is it *likely*?'

Tim looked at the floor. How do you tell a woman that she is known, if at all, for her persuasive and acquiescent ways with old men?

'Oh I *see*.' Her face had tautened, her eyes grown fiery. 'Because it's *me*!'

'No,' he said untruthfully. 'But because you have not spent your life entirely alone. How could you have at – what . . . ?' His voice petered out, anxious not to insult her further.

She laughed – an unmusical sound. 'Don't be shy,' she mocked. 'I'm impervious. You've seen all there is to see. What would you say – twenty-five, thirty-five, forty even?'

He smiled. 'I would say,' he paused, 'thirty-two.'

She clapped her hands. 'Oh *very* good! The perfect gentleman. Just wrong enough to be polite without a suspicion of flattery.'

He shrunk inwardly from her anger, knowing it to come from self-contempt.

The telephone rang. 'Yes,' she said. 'Yes,' an altered tone, respectful yet mocking. 'No, I'm not alone. I have my solicitor here with me. No.' Again. 'No, Sir, I can't do that. It's too late. Well, of course I understand your position.' She rolled her eyes at Tim. 'Of course I won't. Have I ever . . . ?' The indistinct voice droned on. 'I assure you . . . of course . . . but . . .' Her attempts to reply were ineffectual. Finally she put the receiver back with a wry smile. 'Men!' she said. 'From the highest to the lowest, they're all the same. Nothing matters when they want you. But when it's over, it's their reputations that count.'

'An illustrious client?' hazarded Tim.

'Indeed,' she snapped, 'and the higher their rank, the weaker their nerve. It seems I've taken quite a risk in involving the law. A very great risk. And of course . . .' A sudden thought crossed her face. 'Oh Lord! Tim, you'll have to go. I have some urgent telephoning to do.' Faced with this sudden determination, so different from her earlier weakness, Tim hugged her warmly and left without demur.

As soon as she had seen him safely out of her front door, she rushed to the safe concealed behind the electrical plug in her airing cupboard and took out a sheet of paper with a telephone number and a single word. She ran to the telephone and dialled the number. At the answer of an official voice, she gave the word. There was a brief silence and then the voice said, 'You'll be put through directly.' Another pause and then a voice she hadn't heard for three years.

'It's me,' she said.

'I'm so glad,' the voice was warm and welcoming as always. 'Wait while I switch on the scrambler. I never can remember which bloody button.' The line vibrated, then cleared.

'I've heard, of course,' he said.

She laughed. 'I should have guessed that. I was just so worried.'

'Dearest Perky,' said the voice. 'There's nothing to worry about, except what's happened to you. Are you bearing up?'

'Oh yes,' she said, 'but what if . . . ?'

'No!' he said. 'If it comes, it comes. I regret nothing and I still miss you. Politics is a strange business. Now, more importantly, what can *I* do to help you? Have you got a good solicitor?'

'Yes,' she said. 'He's very kind.'

'He'll need to be more than that, I'm afraid. Oh damn! Interruptions this end. Ring me again if you need help. And remember – I'm thinking of you. Let's hope they put the bastard away for a long time!' The line went dead.

Hugging the piece of paper to her breast, she walked slowly back to the little safe. So – not all men were the same. She went back to pour herself some more coffee.

Chapter 28

'All stand!'

The barrage of noise six months later, as the crowd on the gallery benches jostled and gossiped, immediately ceased, and was replaced by scraping sounds as everyone in the courtroom stood up for the judge. He was a slight figure swathed in scarlet, with a large nose and bushy white eyebrows that sprouted voluminously over indistinct eyes. His heavy wig was a model of cleanliness and order.

The assembled lawyers bowed and he acknowledged their courtesy with a languid bow of his own. Tim, seated behind Mr Ridley, looked up at the gallery. In the front row he could see the colossal figure of Lady Woodchester, squeezed between Max Ingram on one side and Jim Lubbock on the other. Flora Knox, crammed into a corner by a mass of donkey-jacketed reporters, waved at him. He smiled back. There was the sudden sound of a single blow of wood on wood.

'Charles Andrew Scrymgeour Chesterfield.'

The Colonel, who had been talking earnestly to a rather thinner Robin Ruggles, stood up.

'You are charged that, on the fifteenth day of November last year, you did commit an offence, namely rape, contrary to section one subsection one of the Sexual Offences Act nineteen fifty-six. How do you plead?'

'Not guilty, my lord.' His voice was strong and clear.

The judge nodded. 'You may be seated,' he said, with something of kindness in his voice. Mr Gregory, who had been thumbing through his papers, looked up sharply as the jurors were called in one by one. But there was no challenge, and they took their oath as a body.

'I swear by Almighty God that I will faithfully try the several issues joined between our Sovereign lady the Queen and the prisoner at the Bar and give a true verdict according to the evidence.'

'No affirmers for once,' muttered Mr Ridley over his shoulder. Tim felt the acid stare of the judge embracing them both and made no reply. The jury sat down in silence. There were nine men and three women.

'Well, Mr Ridley?'

'I appear for the prosecution, my lord, and my learned friend Mr Gregory for the defence.' The judge nodded.

'I shall be calling Miss Metternich to give evidence as to the events of the night in question,' said Mr Ridley, 'and medical evidence to corroborate what she says. It is the Crown's case that the defendant inveigled this young woman into his house and proceeded sexually to assault her, without any encouragement, leading to the offence of rape. Evidence will be given to show that she put up a considerable struggle and that her cries for help went unheeded. I will also show that she reported the crime as soon as she reasonably could, and I shall be calling witnesses as to her distressed state, by way of any further corroboration. Without further delay, I call Miss Metternich.'

Perky walked across the courtroom and stepped into the witness box with her face set in an expressionless mask. She looked immaculate, her severe dove-grey suit accentuating her height rather than her slender but voluptuous figure.

'Take the Bible in your right hand.' The court official had an unexpectedly squeaky voice. 'And repeat the words on this card.'

'I swear by Almighty God.' She paused, and Tim could see her eyes flicker round the room, taking in the Colonel and the familiar faces peering like birds of prey over the balcony parapet opposite. 'That the evidence I shall give,' her voice, also, was strong and relaxed, 'to this court and the jury sworn between our Sovereign lady the Queen and the prisoner at the Bar,' she paused again, and coughed softly, 'shall be the truth, the whole truth and nothing but the truth.'

Mr Ridley walked up to her and smiled encouragingly. She gave him a taut little smile in return, then composed her face and made as if to brush a loose hair off her forehead.

'Your full name is Astrid Amelia Metternich, isn't it?'

'Yes.'

'Will you tell his lordship, in your own words, what happened on the evening of Thursday the fifteenth of November last year?'

For the first time she looked up at the judge, and met his glance without wavering.

'Well,' she said, 'Colonel Chesterfield was well known to me. I had met him on many occasions.'

'Social occasions?'

'Yes. Dinner parties. Ascot. Dances.'

'Had you ever met him privately?'

'Alone, you mean?'

'Yes. Alone.'

There was a pause.

'No,' she said, and the judge's pen squeaked across the page.

'Please go on.'

'As it happens, the Colonel owns the Square behind the mews where I live. There's been quite a lot of trouble going on there over the leases. I'm lucky enough to have the freehold of my house. But I understood he wanted to ask me about my neighbours at the back of my house, who are his tenants. So when he asked me to come round to see him, I saw no reason not to.'

'You didn't think it was an amorous invitation?'

'Certainly not.'

'You anticipated nothing beyond a business meeting?'

'My lord!' Mr Gregory had half risen, putting a querulous tone into his voice.

'Yes. Yes, Mr Gregory. I agree. Mr Ridley, please allow your witness to give us her own story. She seems able to tell it quite clearly without your lead.'

'Thank you, my lord.' Mr Ridley bowed politely. 'Please go on Miss Metternich.'

'I rang the doorbell and the Colonel let me in.'

'Was he alone?'

'Yes.'

'And then?'

'He took my coat and led the way upstairs. His apartment is on the first floor.'

'Did you see anybody else on the way?'

'No.'

'Please go on.'

'The door to his apartment was open. He showed me into a small sitting room overlooking the back of the house.'

'Had he touched you at all?'

'Yes,' she replied, after a moment's thought. 'He had taken my arm to lead me towards the inner room.'

'By the forearm?'

'No,' she said. 'By the upper arm.'

'Will you permit me to demonstrate to his lordship?'

'Yes,' she said, and shuddered as he took hold of her.

'Like this?'

'Yes,' she said.

'Please continue.'

'Well – he gave me a drink. I sat down on the sofa. He sat down beside me.' Her speech was becoming breathy, and she was much paler now, revealing how little make-up she had on. Her ivory skin had an almost greenish tinge. 'He seemed so polite, so normal.'

'I'm very sorry,' said Mr Ridley. 'We all of us here realize what an ordeal this is for you. But the story must be told.'

'He put his hand inside my dress.'

'On your leg?'

'No,' she said. 'My breast.'

'Did you object?'

'Of course. I moved his hand.'

'And?'

'He apologized. In such a nice way. And then he left the room. I was just deciding how best to leave when the door flew open, and he just ran at me. He had no clothes on, just something round his waist.' She sat down, leant forward and rested her head on the shelf of the box.

The judge waited for a moment, and then said gently, 'Miss Metternich, if you would rather give your evidence sitting down, please do so. You said the defendant had something round his waist?'

'Yes, my lord.' She had made a visible effort to control herself.

'Could you be more explicit?'

'It seemed to be some sort of thong. It was black, and I think elastic.'

'Was he excited?' asked Mr Ridley.

'He had an erection, yes.' A sort of satisfied sigh rang round the room, swiftly suppressed.

'And then?'

'Well, of course I jumped up, but he pushed me back on to the sofa. He pulled up my dress, and . . . and . . .'

'You'll have to give us the details, I'm so sorry,' said Mr Ridley.

'I tried to fight him off.'

'You hit him?'

'Certainly. I hit him on the face, I clawed him. But he had the skirt over my head. I managed to get hold of his hair, but he bit my breast so hard that I had to let go.'

'Your right breast?'

'Yes,' she said, her hand moving as if to protect it. 'He jammed one of my legs against a table. I started screaming and punching him. He was much stronger than I expected.'

'Please go on.' The judge was leaning forward as if to try to catch her words. One of the jurors, a young woman with a blue hair band, had begun to weep.

'I felt him enter me. He started shouting at me. I

managed to get hold of his balls and pinched them. I think that's when he came.'

Someone, somewhere, gave a faint cry.

The courtroom was an oasis of silence. Around them the lawcourts buzzed with the contested affairs of men. Outside the building, the streets of London vibrated with the antagonisms of the traffic. But there, in the stifling intensity of the moment, life seemed suspended.

At last Mr Ridley broke the silence. 'There was no doubt that he penetrated you?' he asked in a voice of great tenderness.

She shook her head.

'In shaking your head, you mean . . . ?'

'There was no doubt about it,' she said through gritted teeth.

'What happened then?'

'Oh, he was completely exhausted. I just pushed him off me on to the floor, pulled my dress round me, and ran out into the street.'

'Did you meet anyone?'

'Yes, there was a woman in the hallway.'

'Did you speak to her?'

'No – she shouted something at me and slammed her door.'

'You went home?'

'Yes, of course. I had to wash myself. I soaked and soaked. Then I rang the police.'

'Thank you, my dear. Now that we have the basic picture, I should like to examine one or two points in detail, so that my lord and the jury are in no doubt. When did you first meet Colonel Chesterfield?'

There was a long pause, while she stared blankly past the prosecutor.

'I can't be sure,' she said at length. 'But it might

have been at Lady Woodchester's about eight years ago. I was introduced to him by a friend.'

'Had he ever invited you to anything since then?'

'No.'

'Ever telephoned you, or written to you?'

'Never.'

'Never sent you flowers?'

'Oh no.'

'Or given any sign of sexual inclination towards you?'

'Definitely not.'

'Even though you met him at various social functions.'

'Yes.'

'You own the freehold of your mews house?'

'I do.'

'And the properties at the back of yours, namely Scrymgeour Square, are owned by the Chesterfield Estates Company?'

'Yes. I believe so.'

'How exactly did the Colonel contact you on the evening in question?'

'The telephone rang. I answered it.'

'Did you recognize his voice.'

'No. He sounded like so many others. He said who it was and asked if I could come round to twenty-four Scrymgeour Square to discuss his problems with his tenants.'

'Did you wonder why he was asking you?'

'Yes, I did. But I had some spare time. He's a distinguished man who has always been polite to me. I didn't see why I shouldn't oblige him.'

'Quite so.' If Mr Ridley was dissatisfied with her answer, he gave no sign of it. 'You realize that one of the standard defences against rape is that the victim led her assailant on, encouraging him to believe that she was willing to have sexual intercourse?'

'Yes.'

'Was there any chance, however remote, that the defendant could have believed that you were willing to accept his sexual advances?'

She raised her head, as if to confront the entire courtroom with all its hot perspiring occupants.

'None whatever,' she said loudly.

Mr Ridley sat down.

The judge looked at the clock above the public doors opposite him. 'Mr Gregory,' he said. The elderly barrister rose with an attentive expression. 'It's after half past twelve,' the judge said, 'and no doubt your cross-examination may take some time. I wouldn't want to interrupt your flow.'

'I'm most grateful for your lordship's consideration for my flow,' the barrister replied with an urbane bow. 'Yes, I do expect my cross-examination to be thorough.'

'In that case,' said the judge, 'we will adjourn until two o'clock.'

'All stand!' Proceeded by his marshal, an eager young man with a wispy moustache, the judge edged his way along the bench, stepped nimbly off the dais and vanished behind the oak screen that hid the door into his inner room.

'Coming?'

Tim shook his head to clear the angry thoughts, and then nodded, following Mr Ridley past where Mr Gregory was conferring with Robin Ruggles. Robin did not acknowledge him in any way. He just stared through him.

'It's pretty clear, isn't it?' Tim said.

They sat in the wine bar, devouring generous helpings of lamb chops covered with thick savoury gravy, and washed down with fresh apple juice.

'Oh yes,' said Mr Ridley, one finger exploring his inner ear. 'There's no doubt about the facts.'

'Well then . . . ?'

'It's how you interpret them,' he added with a grin. 'You're a friend of our client's?'

'Yes,' said Tim. 'I am,' ignoring the other's darting glance of speculation.

'How will she hold up to Gregory?'

'You mean . . . ?'

'This afternoon he'll be trying to crucify her. It's their only chance. The Colonel's set for six years at least unless they can shake the jury's confidence in her. It's a pity she's so smartly turned out. I've heard things, of course. But I'm not sure how much he can bring out.'

'Is that relevant?' Tim was suddenly beginning to appreciate what Perky had meant about risk.

'I'll try to stop it, of course,' said the other. 'But I don't think the judge will support us. Hi, Joseph! Come and join us.' Mr Gregory had walked in alone and came over to their table.

'Those chops are exceptional. You know Tim Bryce?'

'How are you?' Mr Gregory looked far more human in his faded grey tweed coat and neat pinstripe trousers.

'What about the by-election then? That's one in the eye for the Prime Minister!' They settled down together, and when Mr Gregory ordered a carafe of Médoc, they relented and joined him in toasting the lucky candidate for Berington.

Back in court, in wig and gown, he was transformed back into a figure of mingled contempt and fear. His wig was offensive in its greasy tangle, and his forehead was shining with sweat, but there was a suppressed violence in his manner as he sorted through his papers for the last time that communicated itself to those who watched him.

'Miss Metternich.'

'Yes,' she said, crossing her legs as he approached her.

'This morning you gave us a lurid, even sensational, account of your evening with my client.'

She continued to look at him without response.

'I should like to take you through those events again.'

Again silence.

'Let me see. You received a telephone call from my client?'

'Yes.'

'Did he actually mention the question of leases?'

She paused. 'I'm not sure.'

'You said, and I quote, "you understood he wanted to ask me about my neighbours." Are you now retracting that?'

'No,' she said. 'That is what I understood. He may not have been specific.'

'Oh I see. You mean he may have said something quite else, but you inferred an interest in your neighbours?'

'Well – yes.'

'Isn't it the case that what he actually said was, "I haven't seen you for ages. Would you like to come round for a drink?"'

'Mmm.' Perky considered this, her head on one side. 'Yes – his first sentence was rather like that.'

'Now we're getting somewhere, Miss Metternich. So off you went, and he met you at the front door?'

'Yes.'

'Remind me what you were wearing.'

'What I was wearing?'

'If you would.'

'Well . . .'

'I'm sure you can remember.'

She gave him a strange look, of half anger, half respect.

'I was wearing a black dress.'

'Short?'

'Knee length.'

'With a high neck?'

'Not particularly.'

'Now don't be modest, Miss Metternich. You're famous for your figure. It was very low cut, wasn't it?'

'It is by Pinzo. It has a low cut.'

'Indeed it has. By good fortune, my lord and the jury can enjoy the effect since I have some enlarged photographs of you wearing the same dress at the Royal Academy Summer Banquet. With your permission, my lord . . . ?'

The judge glanced briefly at Mr Ridley who affected total boredom. The pictures were distributed.

'It suits you, Miss Metternich.'

'I am very grateful for your good opinion, Mr Gregory.'

'But in this picture, forgive me, you don't seem to be wearing a brassiere?'

He handed her the photograph which she studied thoughtfully.

'Do you?' he persisted.

'No,' she said. 'Pinzo's creations rarely require them.'

'In fact, on the evening of November fifteenth, you were wearing no underclothes at all.'

An audible hiss ran round the room. Tim saw Mr Ridley's eyes flicker. But his body remained studiously nonchalant.

'As it happens that is so.'

'As it happens . . . ! Will you tell my lord why not?'

'Certainly. As you can no doubt see, that dress is made of silk jersey. Because it fits so tightly, my underclothes would show up in a way of which I am sure you would disapprove.'

A little ripple of laughter ran round the room. Because she had delivered this response with complete candour, without any sense of playing to the gallery, it had an entirely favourable effect. But Mr Gregory passed on without comment.

'You say the Colonel gave you a drink.'

'Yes.'

'Or did you ask for one?'

'I really can't remember. I think he asked me what I would like.'

'And you said . . . ?'

'I said I should like a glass of champagne.'

'*Indeed*? Champagne.'

'Do you think that wrong?'

'Oh, Miss Metternich. It really doesn't matter what I think. It is what the jury thinks that matters. Now we are getting a clearer picture of that evening appointment, aren't we? There you are, in the Colonel's private sitting room, sipping the champagne that you have asked for, in a dress so tight that you can't wear knickers, and so low that you can't wear a brassiere. It's a tantalizing scene. What must the Colonel have thought of it, a nicely brought-up young lady like you?'

Silence enfolded the room. Tim shifted in his chair, uncomfortably aware of an ache in his back and legs.

'Remind me how you first met the Colonel?'

'I think, though I cannot be sure, that it was at Lady Woodchester's, about seven or eight years ago.'

'So you said. You were introduced to him by a friend.'

'I expect so.'

'You *expect* so. But you told us so on oath. And who was that friend.'

She thought. 'I'm sorry,' she said, shaking her head. 'It's a long time ago.'

'How lucky,' said Mr Gregory, 'that where your memory fails, my client's is still entirely lucid. It was Lord Sennowe, wasn't it?'

'Perhaps.' Her nonchalance was not entirely convincing.

'Perhaps? Oh dear me, no. There's no perhaps about it. However, I shall come back to this later. At the moment I want to pursue your account of the evening.'

He passed and went back to the long table where he had been sitting immediately in front of Robin Ruggles and to the right of the dock where Colonel Chesterfield, by sitting down, could scarcely be seen apart from his head and the tips of his shoulders.

'He placed his hand on your breast.'

'Yes.'

'The right breast?'

She thought.

'Or can't you remember which?'

'He was sitting on my right,' she said. 'His hand came round my back and slipped into my dress. So it must have been the left breast.'

'And you moved it with your hand?'
'Yes.'
'Immediately?'
'Of course.'
'Well, there's no of course about it. But again we'll leave that for the present.'

'My lord!' Mr Ridley had risen and came out from behind the table.

'Yes, Mr Ridley.' The judge looked down at him with just a hint of impatience.

'There seems rather a lot of unnecessary toying with this witness. Something indeed of wholly unjustifiable innuendo in my learned colleague's approach.'

'Well,' said the judge, 'I think we shall just have to let him pursue his own course at this stage.' He returned to writing his notes. After a moment, Mr Ridley returned to his seat.

'Carry on, Mr Gregory,' said the judge without looking up.

'Did you say anything to my client when you extracted your breast from his grip?'
'I don't think so.'
'You didn't say "Not too fast"?'
'Certainly not!'
'With a light laugh?'
'I didn't say anything. But if I had, it would hardly have been with any kind of laugh, least of all a light one.'
'That is your story?'
'It's the truth.'
'Then he got up and left the room?'
'Yes.'
'So, having been fondled in such an intimate way, naturally you fled downstairs?'

'No.'

'No? *No*? After having been sexually assaulted as you tell us?'

'No.'

'In fact you stayed for more?'

'I didn't take it as seriously as I should have.'

'Understandably.'

She stared at him. 'Understandably?' she repeated.

'When my client returned, you say he was wearing nothing but a thong?'

The oldest member of the jury, a stout man with half-moon spectacles, dressed in a thick green jacket, began to make notes.

'Yes.'

'Sexually excited?'

'Yes.'

'The thong was black?'

'Yes.'

'Elastic?'

'Yes.'

'I must say, you're a very observant young lady. You obviously weren't as surprised at this as some might have been.'

She didn't reply.

'There was quite a wrestling match. You seized his testicles. Why was that?'

'I wanted to hurt him, to make him stop.' Her cheeks were red now, red and blotchy.

'You have said your dress was over your head. You were lucky to find them.'

'In my experience,' she snapped, 'they are generally to be found in the same place.'

Several men laughed, but Mr Gregory was beaming at her.

'In your experience. In your experience. Quite so!'

Mr Ridley half rose, but thought better of it. He was drawing an elaborate design of mosaics in full view of the jury box. 'And then, you said, "he came".'

'Yes.'

'Your words.'

'Well what does Mrs Gregory say?' she said, half standing up in her agitation, her voice in an exaggerated caricature of genteel coyness. 'Goodness gracious Mr Gregory I do believe you've shot your load?'

The judge used his hammer on the table to silence the uproar. Tim caught Mr Ridley's despairing glance and stopped grinning.

'Miss Metternich,' said the judge. 'I must ask you to confine yourself to answering Counsel's questions. It is his duty to put these points to you. However distasteful they may be, I must ask you to restrain yourself.'

'I'm very sorry, my lord,' she said meekly, unable to resist the shadow of a wink in Tim's direction.

'Thank you,' said Mr Gregory, 'for showing us a little of the real Perky Metternich. That is the name you answer to, isn't it? Perky?' He put a telling emphasis on the diminutive.

She shrugged. 'One cannot always choose one's own nickname.'

'Just so. I want to return to your first meeting with the Colonel. You were introduced by Lord Sennowe.'

'So you say.'

'I do say so. Lord Sennowe is a friend.'

'Yes.'

'Just a friend?'

'Yes.'

'Oh come now, Miss Metternich. Lord Sennowe was more than just a friend, wasn't he?'

'My lord!'

'Yes, Mr Ridley.'

'It cannot possibly be in the interests of justice or the defendant's case to bandy about the names of people who cannot answer for themselves in this case.'

'Mr Gregory?'

'Well, my lord. I'm afraid I've got rather a long list of names I want to question this witness about.'

'I see. Well, I think the jury had better retire at this point so I can hear the arguments on both sides.'

As the jurors filed out, several showing obvious disappointment, Tim looked up at the gallery to where Flora was sitting. She met his gaze impassively.

'Now Mr Gregory.'

'It is the defence's case, my lord, that Miss Metternich is a young woman whose profession is, to put it bluntly, to sleep with older men in return for large sums of money. I have the names of seven men who I understand have given her considerable sums in return for her favours. This was of course well known to the defendant. He believed her to be visiting him in the normal course of her profession.'

'I see. Mr Ridley?'

'Without conceding any of the defence's scurrilous attacks on this witness's honour and good name, it is well established that the law protects all citizens regardless of their antecedents. As Hale has it "Even that the woman was a common strumpet is no excuse".'

'Well, Mr Gregory?'

'Oh, my lord. Counsel for the prosecution knows as well as I do, my lord, that it is also well established in law and your lordship will be all too familiar with the cases of Banker, Tissington, Greatbanks – I hardly think I need to trot out all the authorities.'

'Your point being?'

'My point being that the prosecution's witness's character is very relevant as far as establishing in the jury's mind the probability or otherwise of her consent, or the reasonableness of my client's assumption of her consent.'

'My lord, I most strenuously protest,' said Mr Ridley. 'A cowardly attack on this witness can serve only to worsen the fearful ordeal she has undergone. Nor presumably do the defence wish to open the door to me, as I certainly should, to uncover the evidence of the defendant's past.'

'Mr Gregory?'

'On the contrary, my lord. My client is perfectly willing to be examined on the whole of his character. Indeed he welcomes the chance to speak openly in the interests of clearing his name. Moreover it is central to the defence that my client, to his misfortune, has some difficulty in – er – achieving full sexual release. This fact would have been well known to Miss Metternich. My client naturally believed her energetic struggles to be evidence of her commitment to earning his goodwill. Indeed, it was precisely because of these struggles that the evening was such a success from his point of view.'

The judge's face was a picture. He stared at Mr Ridley, Mr Ridley stared back. They were both at a loss for words.

'I see,' said the judge at last, shaking his head. 'I see.'

Mr Ridley raised his eyes and turned to Tim. There was no hiding the baffled sense of defeat in his expression.

'Mr Ridley.'

'Yes, my lord.'

'I think I'm going to permit Mr Gregory's line of questioning.'

'As your lordship pleases.'

The jury returned to their box. The two older women looked tired, the younger one had an angry expression on her angular face. Perky, who had also retired, returned to the stand. She looked at no-one.

'Miss Metternich. Lord Sennowe was your lover.'

'Do I have to answer, my lord?' she appealed direct to the judge.

'I'm afraid so,' he said, bowing his head sympathetically.

'Yes, he was.'

'Starting from the age of seventeen.'

'Yes.'

'When he was fifty-two.'

'Yes.'

There was something of a scuffle as three of the reporters made for the gallery door, clambering over their neighbours.

'He gave you a great deal of money?'

'He was a generous friend.'

'I repeat. He gave you a great deal of money?'

'Yes.'

'And Mr James Fortnum.'

'Yes.'

'He gave you a great deal of money?'

'Yes.'

'And Sir Edgar Turnbull?'

'Yes.' Lady Woodchester's intake of breath was prodigious.

'He gave you a great deal of money?'

'Yes.'
'Mr Ernest Grazheim?'
'Yes.'
'Lord John Wharton?'
'Yes.'
'They both gave you a great deal of money?'
'Yes!'
'I have two other names on this piece of paper which I will show to you and to his lordship. The reason for not giving them in open court will be self-evident.'

He showed her the paper and then walked over and handed it up to the judge who looked at it and put it aside without comment.

'They were both your lovers?'
'Yes.'
'They both gave you a great deal of money?'
'Yes.'
'You must be a very rich young woman?'
'Money is relative.'
'Indeed. I don't suppose you have any figures handy, but it is a matter of public record that the Channel Island Company of which you are the sole shareholder paid three-point-one-four million pounds for the freehold of 141-148 Wolfgangstrasse – a large building in Frankfurt, my lord.'

She shrugged. 'I am well advised.'
'In financial matters, perhaps. Now, Miss Metternich. Can you help us? What my lord and the jury are interested to know is this. Why did these men give you quite so much money?'
'Why does anyone give gifts?'
'It was to buy your sexual services, wasn't it?'

She paused and considered. Then she raised her head and looked straight at her prosecutor. It was a strange look, not angry, not defiant, certainly not ashamed nor for that matter showing the disdain with which some women treat the enslavement of the male by the female. It was a thoughtful, even tender look.

'Yes,' she said. 'I expect so. I like to think that they felt there was an exchange of generosity.'

'Or indeed bodily fluids?'

'My lord!' Mr Ridley's shout of anger was echoed by at least one of the jurors, the man with the spectacles, who muttered something inarticulate.

'Yes, indeed. Mr Gregory. I really don't think that remark was worthy of you.'

'I apologize, my lord. I do indeed.' He paused to collect his thoughts. If he was angry with himself for losing valuable ground for the pleasure of a gibe, he didn't show it. 'In fact, Miss Metternich, you are an expensive whore.'

She shrugged again. 'If you choose to call me so.'

'A woman whose body was available for hire, regardless of the age of your clients?'

'Certainly not.'

'Oh, indeed?'

'Of course I chose my friends.'

'A choosy whore?'

'Like most people who can afford to.'

'Well, I don't think we will pursue your philosophy at the Crown's expense, thank you. I want to ask you now about Colonel Chesterfield. You knew of his sexual reputation?'

'Not especially.'

'Oh come now, Miss Metternich. There was a widely publicized court case last year. Everyone knew the Colonel enjoyed, indeed needed, chastisement.'

She glanced across at the defendant and shuddered. 'I really didn't take much notice. But yes, I remember people talking about that.'

'So there you were, nearly naked, upstairs in his flat, drinking his champagne and not making much of a fuss when he fondled your bare breast. What on earth did you expect?'

'I'll tell you,' she cried with sudden vehemence. Tim clenched his fists. 'I expected the protection of the law that anyone, man or woman, might ask against violent self-gratification. Your client is a monster. A disgusting filthy degraded monster.' She had long since stood up and was shouting over Mr Gregory's vain protests that she be silent. Then just as suddenly, she sat down, dry eyed, docile.

'Well!' said Mr Gregory. 'What an exhibition. Now I should like to proceed with my cross-examination.' She nodded listlessly. 'Why didn't you tell your lurid tale to the woman downstairs?'

'She slammed her door in my face.'

'Or to the people in the street?'

'There was no-one in the street.'

'No-one at all?' His tone was silky.

'Ah!' she said. 'Yes. There *was* a traffic warden. Across the street. I remember now. I certainly wasn't going to tell him.'

'Why not?'

'Because I wanted to wash myself out.'

'That's all.' Mr Gregory sat down.

'Mr Ridley?'

'Just two questions on what we've heard. 'That dress you were wearing, Miss Metternich. Was it for a special occasion?'

She nodded, seeing his point. 'Yes,' she said. 'I was

due to go out to dinner with an old friend. It was as I was getting ready that the Colonel telephoned.'

'So it was pure chance, or rather mischance, that you should have been dressed so decoratively when you kept this tragic appointment?'

She nodded. 'Yes. I'm afraid so.'

'Thank you. Now tell me, Miss Metternich, after you had bathed yourself, was there any delay before you rang the police?'

'None.'

'You spoke to no-one first?'

'No-one.'

'You reported the crime immediately.'

'Immediately.'

After Mr Ridley had sat down, the judge adjourned the Court until the following morning.

Chapter 29

'More soup?'

'No thank you. It was delicious.'

Tim had had a longstanding dinner invitation with Lady Woodchester and had thought it worthwhile not to cancel it. One reward was that, as his official fiancée, Laura was placed beside him; another was the warmth of her thigh against his. He turned to her now.

'You never came to the court.'

'I'm sorry,' she said. 'I couldn't bear to see it. My father told me some of it.' Max Ingram was across the table from Tim, on their hostess's right. They were laughing about something.

'She put up a sterling fight.'

'You mean for someone on very thin ice?' One development within herself had taken her by surprise, her seething anger towards Tim's previous involvements.

'Yes. I'm afraid Gregory had to go for her.'

'What will the papers say?'

'I should think they'll print it verbatim.'

'Daddy wouldn't tell me who the two anonymous men were.' This, of course, was the Subject.

'Perhaps he doesn't know.'

'Do you?'

'Yes.'

'Oh? Can you whisper them to me?'

Tim leant towards her.

'What are you two being so confidential about?' boomed Lady Woodchester. 'No secrets at my table!'

'I was repeating some of Perky Metternich's comments in court.'

'Ugh! That extraordinary young woman! I wonder if we will ever see her again. What do you think, Max?' she added maliciously.

Laura's father met her gaze with an innocent air.

'Good heavens,' he said. 'I really couldn't say. I hardly knew her in any case.'

On Laura's other side was an Appeal Court judge, a tall man with piercing eyes, short ginger hair and thin red lips.

'Now then, Sir Thomas,' she said gaily, catching a flicker of sexual appraisal as he turned to face her. 'What are we poor women to do when we try to accommodate men's goatish tendencies only to find that our generosity is flung in our face if we get raped?'

'Now, don't bully the judge,' shouted her father. 'You know he can't comment on a case in progress.'

'Even so,' persisted Laura, flapping her eyelashes at the judicial lion, 'how are girls like Perky expected to find justice?'

'My dear,' said the old man with a smile that was courteous without being patronizing, 'We judges swear to administer justice according to the law, not the law according to justice. This is a distinction,' he added, making a manful attempt to keep his eyes on her face, 'not readily identified by the general public.'

Alone in her bedroom, three streets away, Perky sat looking into her mirror. She was naked, and the livid scar on her breast shone like a brand even though the lights were turned down low. All her life, she had determined to live by her wits, to submit herself to no test other than her own judgement, sometimes framed on impulse, sometimes on a careful analysis of the issues involved. Perhaps she had been lucky to have escaped public notoriety before. Now she was uncomfortably aware of the journalists camped in the mews outside, waiting for a photograph or a story when she showed herself.

Part of her was excited, or at least disturbed, by the attention she knew she would now incur, not just for a week but for perhaps the rest of her life. Another, bigger, part was sorry for the doors that she knew must now be closed against her. She also had time to pity the men named in court who would themselves already be facing the ridicule or criticism of their families for such public attention as would now focus on their private lives. She smiled sourly at the thought of the two hidden names. How many women in her position had had the responsibility of protecting the reputations of both a Prince and a Prime Minister?

Clearly it was over. She was rich, far richer than Mr Gregory could have anticipated. But what on earth had it all been for? Those besotted men, with their sagging bellies and rotting teeth! Who would come to her parties? Who would share her comedies, now that she was exposed as a common prostitute? She gazed at the woman in the mirror, slim, lithe, heavy breasted, with a limpid olive skin unmarked except for that discoloured stigma. Her neck was very fine, she thought, and so were her teeth.

The doorbell rang and she started. After a pause, she rose to go towards the curtain, but remembered in time. Those reporters! She stood still and waited. The bell rang again. Then loud knocking. With a shrug, she picked up the yellow kimono lying across the chaise longue and hurried downstairs.

'Who is it?' she called out.

'Me.'

'And who's me?' The arrogance of men was past belief.

'Dapper.' A flashlight momentarily flared through the opaque glass above the front door. 'Let me in.' They had not met since Tim's lunch party, since neither had had the courage to face up to their feelings. She struggled with the chain, and opened the door, taking care to stand behind it, so that the bursts of light from the photographers illuminated only Dapper's back as he strode in and slammed the door behind him.

'This is a very public show of support,' she said. 'At least let me get you a drink.'

'Thanks,' he said. 'Some whisky would be reviving.'

'Glenmorangie?'

'Yeah. And some ice if you've got it.'

She slipped behind the oriental screen that hid the doors into her kitchen and the deep drinks cupboard that housed a very wide selection of bottles. If it was her allure that brought men to her in the first place, it was the care she took of their comforts, both physical and digestive, that kept them coming back. She poured out two generous portions and piled the glasses with ice.

While he waited, Dapper eyed the thick Savonnerie rug, the tapestried chairs, the heavy gilt side tables and the little Dali over the mantelpiece. To just such a room had he gone downstairs each night in his childhood to spend an hour with his mother before ascending again to the nursery regime. He felt a cosy womb-like comfort in such opulence and settled himself deeper into the thick velvet of the sofa.

'That's wonderful,' he said appreciatively as Perky handed him the aromatic drink.

'It's nice of you to come. I was feeling very low.'

He shot her a swift glance. 'That's not like you. You seem so positive, so capable.'

She laughed. 'Oh well, the façade is holding up. That's good.' She took a gulp of the liquid. 'Sorry about the reception committee.'

'Oh,' he said. 'I'm used to that after my own little court case.'

'Really?'

'I'd be in prison now if Tim hadn't sorted it out for me. He's a really good friend.'

'Yes,' she said.

'He's one man who will stick by you, you can be sure of that.'

'Yes,' she said, injecting more warmth into her voice, 'although that almost amounts to defamation after today's events.'

Dapper shrugged. 'You and I,' he said, 'accept that there is merit in experience.'

She grinned and took another sip of the whisky. 'And you?' she said. 'Has Tim sorted everything out?'

Dapper laughed. 'Oh no!' he said. 'But at least he's kept me out of bankruptcy for the next few weeks. Which is something, you must admit. I'm not sure what to do next. I'm seriously thinking of South Africa. I had quite a good six years in the army, and in fact I've got some cousins out there who say I might find a job in security or what have you.' He emptied his glass and put it down carefully on the table. 'Anyway,' he added. 'I just dropped in to wish you well. Don't let the buggers get you down.' He stood up. 'You know, Perky,' he moved close to where she too had risen, and held her by the waist, 'if I hadn't made such a muddle of things, I'd have been besieging this little house with whole trunkloads of hard currency.'

She stood speechless. He bent down and kissed her softly on both cheeks, then turned and walked towards the door.

'Dapper,' she said. He turned and mimed a farewell kiss. 'Please stay.'

He stared at her, his yellow eyes puzzled, even a little vulnerable. 'No more whisky,' he said. 'I have to drive north. I have some goodbyes to say. Old tenants, that sort of thing.'

'I need you.'

He smiled. 'You'll manage.'

'Please stay.'

He took her hands. 'You must know that the poor have their pride. I cannot accept for free what I can no longer afford.'

'Oh dear,' she said. 'I can see we're in for a difficult time. You think I'm offering you a romp upstairs.' Again his eyes creased with confusion. 'You give me something I really want, which is kindness. If you are as indifferent to society as you pretend, I can give you something you need in return.'

'Indeed?' He spoke in an icy tone.

'Stop being so *obtuse*,' she shouted. 'I'm asking you to marry me!'

'To marry you?'

'Yes!'

'To *marry* you?'

She began to falter under his astounded gaze. Was it such a shameful idea? Was she so distasteful?

'But you don't understand,' he said. 'I love you. I love you. Don't cry. Please don't cry.' She had run to him and was clinging to him, she was saying something indistinctly. 'What? I can't hear,' he said, leading her to the sofa and sitting down beside her.

'I said – I'll try to love you. I really will.'

'Well then,' he said, passing a hand over his head, his thoughts in total turmoil, 'well then.' Her hand had snaked round his neck and now she pulled his head down on to hers so that she could kiss him. While he drank in her fragrance, he felt her loosening his clothes, pulling them off him, caressing and ultimately guiding him into her, without once removing her lips from his.

'Sounds like he's getting lucky,' remarked the man from the *Sunday Express*, cocking his ear, as his colleague from the *Sun* moodily stamped on his tenth cigarette that night. 'She's got quite a nerve, that girl. I'll give her that.'

'That's about all you ever will give her!' muttered the other. 'Some blokes have all the luck. You could tell he was one of her millionaires just by looking at him.'

Chapter 30

'This will have to be a short meeting, since I am needed in court at ten.' Robin Ruggles, his face still red but strangely shrunken, his neck so thin now that it protruded from his outsize collar like the wrinkled limb of a tortoise, was sitting staring across his father's desk at the demure figure of Flora, her lightweight summer jersey buttoned right up to her chin.

'You asked me to be here at eight,' she said, 'and here I am.'

For the fifth or sixth time, he consulted his wristwatch. 'Yes, indeed.' Silence fell. 'It's a very delicate matter,' he said at last. She waited patiently. 'Very delicate indeed.'

'Is there any chance of a cup of tea?' she said. 'I had to leave Willesden too early to have breakfast.'

He shook his head. 'I'm afraid I don't have any help at the moment,' he said, 'and I haven't quite mastered the art myself. I won't keep you long.' She shrugged and waited again. Having never been to these offices before, the bare patches on the walls where pictures, now at Sotheby's, once hung meant nothing to her. The Colonel was Robin's only remaining client, presumably hanging on as this was hardly an opportune moment for changing solicitors. If Robin's dream had been to have sole control of the business, it had, like the Delphic predictions of ancient Greece, been fulfilled in unexpected fashion. He was captain now, but of an unmasted and sinking ship, long since deserted by his crew.

'You were in court yesterday?' he said, trying to smile, but producing instead the mere caricature of warmth. She nodded. 'The Colonel was very sorry to lose your companionship.' She continued to look straight at him as he spoke. 'Would I be right in assuming you would not wish to resume your arrangement?'

'You would.'

'Ah.' Robin wiped his forehead with his hand, and surreptitiously rubbed it on his trouser leg. The telephone began to ring. He lifted the receiver, without affecting the noise. He pressed first one button, and then another.

'Hello?' The ringing continued, and finally ceased. He slammed the receiver down. 'Bloody machines never work,' he muttered. 'Now! I must get on. The Colonel wants to mark your long and, he hopes, mutually satisfactory association with a small present.'

If he had expected an effusive response, or indeed any sign that Flora had heard, he was disappointed. 'I have here,' he persevered, 'a cheque in your favour for five thousand pounds.' He held the piece of paper firmly beneath one heavy florid hand. 'There is however one small condition attached to its transfer . . .' He waited for encouragement, got none, and continued, 'Which is that you should sign a contract binding yourself not to communicate in any way with any publications whether here or overseas. You appreciate that the Press will inevitably even now be searching for material of a scandalous nature. The only surprising thing is that nothing has occurred before. I have in fact,' he tried another smile, with even less success, 'been searching for you since December!'

'But it has,' she said.

'What has?'

'I am currently considering two offers, one from the *Sun* and one from the *Daily Mirror*.'

'Indeed?'

'Since time is short,' said Flora, who was nothing if not a quick thinker, and from whose agile brain these imaginary negotiations had suddenly sprung as the solution to Max's immediate financial embarrassment, 'let me help by saying I shall happily sign your contract in return for a cheque for £110,000, which matches my best offer so far, and two open Club Class return air tickets to Pisa.' Robin's mouth had dropped open.

'Pisa?' he repeated.

'Yes,' she said. 'I want to spend the winter in Italy. It will help keep me out of the public eye, since a certain amount of all this is of course public knowledge.'

'I hardly think,' said Robin, his voice hardening as the scale of the demand sank in, 'that the Colonel will agree such terms.'

'Just let me know after the Court rises this evening, will you?' she said sweetly. 'I have to give my response to the others tonight. Of course, I would far rather accommodate your client.' She left, avoiding his proferred hand.

When she and Max arrived at the courtroom, they were met by a harassed Robin who handed her two envelopes; one contained a cheque for the full amount, the other contained a travel agent's voucher for the tickets. She signed his contract on the back of Max's copy of *Country Life*, and the transaction was complete. Neither of the men said a word to the other.

Colonel Chesterfield was in the middle of taking the oath when Tim slipped into his place behind Mr Ridley. Evidence had already been given on behalf of the prosecution by the police sergeant who had taken Perky's call, by the policewoman who had taken her statement, and by the two doctors who had subsequently examined her. All their testimony confirmed that her behaviour was entirely as would be anticipated from the victim of a rape, and that her physical condition showed that it had been an unusually violent assault. It was now Mr Gregory's turn to present the defence.

'You are Colonel Charles Andrew Scrymgeour Chesterfield, of Chesterfield Hall, Staffordshire and twenty-four Scrymgeour Square?'

'I am.'

'You are the holder of the Distinguished Service Order, the Military Cross, and are a Deputy Lieutenant for Staffordshire?'

'I am.'

'You are a magistrate?'

'Yes.'

'For how long?'

The Colonel paused, and thought. 'Thirty-three years,' he said at last.

'So you are familiar with the responsibilities of the Law.'

'Indeed.'

'Well, well. I think we have the picture. Now let's take his lordship and the ladies and gentlemen of the jury through the events as alleged. When did you first meet Miss Metternich?'

'At Lady Woodchester's. She used to give a ball every summer on the eve of the Chelsea Flower Show. Indeed she still does . . .' he added with a sidelong acknowledgement to the beaming old battleaxe in the gallery. She waved back with unselfconscious glee.

'You seem very certain of the occasion?'

'Oh yes. You see she was an object of considerable interest. Rupert Sennowe had kept her out of sight for several years. This was the first time I had a chance to see her. Her concealment had added appreciably to her cachet as what my grandmother would have called a *grande horizontale*.'

Mr Ridley showed some signs of restlessness, and Mr Gregory made great play of waiting to see if he wished to interrupt. When no such intervention occurred he turned back to his client.

'And your impression?'

'A very alluring young lady.'

'And in the intervening years?'

'We met occasionally. Whenever her current protector asked for her to be invited.'

'You understood her to be kept by these men?'

'Yes indeed. I don't think there was any secret about that.'

'I see.' Mr Gregory looked round at the jury as if to establish that no protest had come from the prosecution. 'Now, coming to the evening of the fifteenth of November. You telephoned her?'

'Yes, I did. I had heard a rumour that she was currently unattached and, to be frank, I wanted to form a liaison with her.'

'Did you anticipate any problem?'

'No.'

'As simple as that?'

'Well, I am fortunate enough to be able to meet what I anticipated would be a substantial demand for money.'

'You based this assumption on what?'

'On conversations with previous supporters.'

'How did you phrase your invitation?'

'I said that I was on my own, hadn't seen her for ages, and wondered whether she would like to come round for a drink.'

'Did you mention leases?'

'Only by way of small talk. Johnnie Wharton said it was important to keep the conversation flowing.'

'Did she accept?'

'Immediately.'

'She didn't mention anything about a later engagement?'

'My lord!'

'Yes, Mr Ridley. I agree. Please don't lead your witness, Mr Gregory.'

'Well, well. Colonel, tell us this, did she say anything else during that conversation?'

The Colonel squared his shoulders. 'Nothing at all.'

'Not on any subject?'

'No.'

'So, there you were, waiting to propose an amorous alliance, and in she came.'

'Quite so.'

'In the dress which I am showing you now?'

The Colonel peered at the photograph, paused and took out a pair of thick spectacles. He put them on and smiled. 'Yes,' he said, looking up. 'It suits her, doesn't it?'

'And what did you conclude from her appearance?'

'That she was ready for action.'

The young woman in the jury box gave an audible hiss.

'What then?'

'Well, I offered her a drink. She asked for some champagne, so I went and opened a bottle I had in the fridge. Then we sat down on the sofa.'

'You put your arm around her?'

'Yes.'

'You put your hand on her breast?'

'Well, you've seen the dress. Where else was I to put it?' The Colonel chuckled at his own joke. The courtroom remained largely silent apart from a few sniggers from the gallery.

Mr Gregory frowned. 'What was her reaction?'

'Well, I had been handling an iced bottle. Naturally she moved it. But I think, by the time one reaches my age, one can tell when a woman wants one. So I went next door to get ready.'

'In so far as?'

'Well,' the Colonel coughed, and looked at the judge.

'Please go on, Colonel. We all understand what an ordeal this must be for you.' Mr Ridley made loud scratching sounds with his pen.

'Well,' said the Colonel again. 'I was rather badly wounded at Arnhem, so I generally prefer getting ready by myself.'

'The prosecution produced evidence about an elastic black thong.'

'Yes,' the old man said uncomfortably. 'It – er – conceals and, well, helps.'

'I think,' said Mr Gregory 'that you had better explain to the Court about your sexual problems.'

Another hush settled on the room. The judge took off his spectacles and laid them beside his notebook.

The jury, in a body, shifted their gaze to the ceiling, to the stenographer, to any spot other than the defendant's face.

'Um,' he said at last. 'Since my operation – prostate, you know – it hasn't been easy. A bit of spanking, that sort of thing, helps.'

'It got you into trouble before, didn't it?'

'It did indeed, Mr Gregory,' said his client earnestly. 'And you were the prosecutor!' A burst of general laughter released the tension in the room. Even the judge smiled.

'But you were fully acquitted of any guilt, weren't you?' said the barrister with a mock-deprecating grin.

'I certainly was.'

'So you embraced Miss Metternich on the sofa?'

'Yes.'

'Did she show any signs of resistance?'

'None whatever.'

'She didn't cry for help?'

'Not for help. She did, I'm glad to say, show signs of enjoying our romp.'

'Did she hit you?'

'Oh yes. She'd obviously done her homework.'

'By which you mean?'

'That my difficulties were well known. She knew what I wanted. Johnnie Wharton said . . .' He tailed off.

'Go on.'

'No,' he said decisively. 'I shouldn't repeat that sort of thing.'

'I'm sure your self-restraint does you great credit,' said Mr Gregory, 'in view of the precarious and embarrassing situation in which this woman has placed you.'

The Colonel smiled at his feet.

'And afterwards?'

'Afterwards she left, I suppose.'

'You suppose?'

'Well, it was such a splendid occasion from my point of view, that I'm afraid that I must have dropped off.'

'And what woke you up?'

'The police arriving to arrest me.'

Mr Gregory paused. 'Did this surprise you?'

'Well of course it did.'

'You had no reason to expect them?'

'No, of course not.'

'So, if I may paraphrase your evidence, you knew Miss Metternich to be available for sex in exchange for money, you invited her round, you engaged in sexual congress with her during which she showed precisely that degree of violence that you believed she knew was necessary for your gratification, and then she left. End of story?'

'Well, no,' said the Colonel.

'No?' This was clearly not the answer that Mr Gregory had either anticipated or desired. 'No?'

'No, no. I thought it was the *beginning* of the story. I hoped ours would be a long and mutually satisfactory relationship.'

'I see,' breathed the relieved barrister. 'I *see*.' He sat down.

Mr Ridley continued to write for some seconds. Then he looked up to meet the judge's inquisitive gaze. 'Yes, my lord,' he said unhurriedly. 'I am so sorry.' He rose.

'Colonel Chesterfield.' The older man watched him impassively. 'You're becoming quite a figure in the Law Courts.' The Colonel shrugged and

Mr Gregory made a great mime of thinking this sally extremely amusing. 'Have you ever been married?'

'No, sir.'

'Would you care to tell us why?'

The Colonel creased his eyes, staring past the judge. 'I suppose,' he said, 'I never met a woman I felt able to ask to share my life.'

'Or is it because you see women as a route to instant sexual gratification rather than as independent beings worthy of respect?'

'That's a bit too highbrow for me,' said the Colonel with a thin smile.

'Let's deal first with the telephone call.' Mr Ridley was now standing directly confronting the defendant. 'When you talked about these leases.'

'I didn't talk about them,' said the Colonel. 'I mentioned the trouble I was having.'

'By way of small talk?'

'Exactly.'

'The sort of subject any girl might be ecstatic to hear about?'

'I had an idea that *this* girl might, since she has such a pronounced interest in the world of property.'

If Mr Ridley felt the Colonel had scored, he gave no sign of it. 'I want to explore now your methods of wooing,' he said. 'Did you ask Miss Metternich if she was willing to make love to you?'

'No,' said the Colonel.

'Do you not consider that an essential prerequisite?'

'Not for a girl of Miss Metternich's profession.'

'Leaving aside the scurrilous nature of that reply, are you expecting the Court to take the view that no experienced woman is permitted a choice in partners?'

'No,' said the Colonel thoughtfully. 'No, I don't. But Miss Metternich and I understood each other.'

'You have heard her testify to the contrary.'

'Yes.'

'So she is lying?'

'Yes.'

'And what was the price?'

'I beg your pardon?'

'What was the price of her compliance?'

'I don't understand you.'

'Come, come, Colonel. You understand me perfectly well. You have characterized Miss Metternich as a whore. You have testified that you knew she demanded payment for sex. What price did she demand from you?' Strangely, it seemed that neither the Colonel nor his advisers had anticipated this line of questioning. He stared down at Mr Gregory. Mr Gregory half turned in his chair, stared back. Suddenly Tim saw in the old barrister's face something he had not expected to see. It was not far from laughter. It was as if Mr Gregory was enjoying his client's discomfort.

'It went without saying.'

'*It went without saying,*' repeated Mr Ridley. 'Dear me, Colonel. If that is how you negotiate the leases of your property, no wonder you are so embroiled in litigation. And yet I'm told you are a very good businessman, well able to negotiate a contract in advance.'

Pausing just long enough for the inconsistency to register with the jury, Mr Ridley moved on. 'I want you to tell me what she cried out during the time you were penetrating her.'

The Colonel shook his head.

'I must insist, Colonel. His lordship will tell you that you must answer my questions.'

The Colonel glared at him. 'No gentleman would ask such a question,' he said coldly.

'Oh well,' said Mr Ridley cheerfully, 'I am perfectly willing to concede that, if you are to be considered the pattern. Now kindly answer the question.'

'Her cries were entirely inarticulate.'

'She begged you to stop!'

'No.'

'She cried for mercy!'

'No.'

'She screamed for help!'

'No.'

'I put it to you that your last three answers have been wholly untrue.'

'No.'

While Mr Ridley vainly flailed around the witness's intransigent certainties, Tim's attention wandered, distracted perhaps by the heat of the courtroom and by the persistent buzzing of a wasp exploring the Gothic cupola in the centre of the ceiling. For a time he watched Perky, now sitting on a wide bench by the side of the stenographer, with a couple of law students taking notes beside her. Up in the gallery, Lady Woodchester had fallen asleep, and Max Ingram was clearly engaged on a crossword puzzle. Even the jurors looked tired and bored. He must have dozed off, because he felt his head jerking back from a nodding position in time to see a new witness taking the stand.

'You are Mrs Jemima Huddleston?'

The second witness turned out to be the tenant of the flat below the Colonel's. She was an emaciated woman, with thin bloodless cheeks and deep lines round her mouth, implying a perpetual scowl.

'You are the tenant of Flat four, twenty-four Scrymgeour Square?' Mr Gregory's tone was cautious, wheedling.

'Joint-tenant. With my husband.'

'Quite so. Now I want to take you back over the events of Thursday the fifteenth of November if I may.' He paused to satisfy himself that she was clear what he was talking about. 'You were in that evening?'

'Oh yes. My husband was having one of his turns, so I had to stay in to wait on him.'

'Do you recall hearing anything in the early evening?'

'I remember that tart arriving.'

'My lord!' Mr Ridley jumped to his feet.

'Yes, yes, Mr Ridley,' said the judge with almost a smile. 'Mrs Huddleston.'

'Yes, my lord?'

'Could you give us your evidence in just plain facts, without any embellishment.'

'Well, there's nothing plainer than that. She was just spilling out of her dress.'

'Mrs Huddleston!' Mr Gregory, not wishing to antagonize the judge, intervened. 'We quite understand. Now why did you notice the prosecution's witness arriving?'

'Because she rang the Colonel's bell. You can hear everything that goes on up there. Doesn't have proper carpets, you see. These old houses are all the same.'

'Did you go out into the hall?'

'Certainly not. I heard him come down to let her in. His man goes out after tea. And I watched her through our peephole.'

'Had you ever seen her before?'

'Dozens of times.' This was a sensation. The whole courtroom resounded with gasps and whispers, even some laughter. Mr Ridley's mouth was sagging with consternation. Tim looked across at Colonel Chesterfield, who had been writing notes in his blank diary. He too was staring at the old woman.

'Dozens of times?' enquired Mr Gregory, hardly able to believe his good fortune.

'Oh yes,' she said grimly, enjoying the effect of her words.

The judge leant forward and peered at her. 'Now let me get this absolutely clear for the jury, Mrs Huddleston,' he said. 'You had seen Miss Metternich calling on the Colonel before?'

'Oh yes, your lordship. Her or others like her.'

Another ripple of sound ran round the room. Mr Gregory turned away in disgust. 'Mrs Huddleston,' he said grimly. 'I must ask you to be precise. My question was – had you ever seen Miss Metternich before?'

'They're all the same, aren't they?' she replied with more than matching austerity. 'Painted trollops, every one of them. There's the one who used to live there, skulking up there in the gallery.' She had stood up and was pointing with fine drama at the seat where Flora was vainly trying to look inconspicuous. 'You was the noisiest of the lot!' the old woman shrieked. 'How do you expect folks like us to get a decent night's sleep with all that caterwauling going on above our heads?' She turned back to the judge who was hiding his mouth behind the judicial hand. 'I tell you, my lord. It was like living in the zoo, with that old rhinoceros snorting and bellowing away and those filthy harlots doing dirty things with him.'

'Mrs Huddleston!' shouted Mr Gregory. 'Please try to settle down and answer my question.'

All at once she subsided. 'No,' she said, 'I don't think I ever did see that last one before. She had a bit more style than the others. A bit less common, if you know what I mean?'

Mr Gregory wiped his brow and then wiped his hand on the bottom of his trousers. 'Now then,' he said, 'did you hear anything strange later on?'

'No!' she replied. 'Just the usual.'

'In short, nothing to suggest that the Colonel was raping the girl?'

'No,' she said shortly.

'And when she came downstairs?'

'She looked as if she'd been having a whale of a time, I can tell you.'

'And did she speak to you?'

'No.'

'She didn't ask you to call the police?'

'No.'

'Nor a doctor?'

'Nor a nurse. Nor a psychiatrist which is what my husband says he needs, that old goat . . .'

'Quite so, thank you Mrs Huddleston,' and Mr Gregory sat down.

Mr Ridley approached her with some caution. 'Now, Mrs Huddleston. We've established you hadn't seen Miss Metternich before. But I want you to tell me exactly what you did hear that evening. And I want you to tell me in as much detail as you can. We're in no hurry, but I am sure that you and your husband would want to see justice done.'

'Oh yes, sir.'

'Good. Now tell my lord when you first became aware of noises above.'

She sat and thought for a moment. Something was bothering her. She looked at the Colonel several times.

'Well?' coaxed Mr Ridley, lowering his voice.

She heaved a great sigh. She had evidently overcome some great internal obstacle. 'Well, it was this screaming.' Her eyes were screwed up, remembering.

'Screaming?' Mr Ridley's throat tightened as a sense of accelerating excitement dominated him. 'Screaming?'

'Oh yes. She was fairly hollering.'

'Did you hear any words?'

'Just "Help!", "Help me!", "Please God help me!" over and over again.'

The courtroom was hushed. Robin Ruggles was slumped with his head in his hands.

'And why didn't you help her, Mrs Huddleston?' Mr Ridley asked in a soft, almost pleading voice.

'Well, honestly, my lord. Look what happened the last time I called the police. The Colonel threatened to have us evicted. We're very fortunate to have a protected tenancy in that area. My husband's none too well, not that he doesn't make it worse sometimes. That's why he can't give evidence here. Not that he'd be any use, having been under his pain killers all evening.'

'I think that's all we need to hear, thank you Mrs Huddleston.' And Mr Ridley went back to his seat.

Those who had been watching Perky's face had watched a gradual and shocking transformation from her habitual calm façade. The skin had tightened over her forehead during the first part of Mrs Huddleston's evidence and the contrast with her pallor had made her eyes seem more luminous. But when the older woman had repeated what she had heard with such singular lack of humanity, great silent tears had begun running down Perky's face, spilling out of her eyes as if fugitives from the pain within. But never once did she falter, before all those other eyes, prurient, avid, pitying, concupiscent eyes, that multiplied around the courtroom, sparkling with excitement or with sympathetic tears to match her own.

'Here.' It was actually Mr Gregory who walked over to her, ignoring those eyes and the thoughts behind them, and took out a shabby pink silk handkerchief. 'Use this.' She took it and smiled.

Without hesitating, he strode back to Mrs Huddleston and bowed towards the judge. 'I have no further questions, my lord.'

No-one had imagined that he had, and those who knew him well knew that he had washed his hands of his client, even though they also knew that he would continue to fight his battle as best he could.

Chapter 31

'Charles Andrew Scrymgeour Chesterfield.' The court was glowing with shafts of brilliant yellow light that pierced through the cupola's panes and lit features here and there, leaving adjacent areas unexpectedly sombre in contrast. One such feature was the defendant's waistcoat, his gold chain sparkling in the sunshine, while his face, protected by one of the cupola's main panels, seemed dark and indistinct.

'You have been found guilty as charged by the unanimous verdict of the jury. I have heard testimony as to your distinguished career, both as a soldier and as a landowner, together with your work for various charities.

'It has been suggested that these should mitigate your sentence for a crime the details of which have now been established. To counter this, there is first the press speculation that your position should have called for a greater sense of responsibility and thus blame. I take no account of that whatsoever. There is the second suggestion that your deliberate attempts to vilify your victim's character have made the offence all the more serious. With this I wholeheartedly agree. Not content with raping this young woman, you have cold-bloodedly set out to destroy her credibility and self-respect.

'I sentence you to seven years' imprisonment. Take him down!'

'It's a great pity,' said the judge that evening, as he stretched out his legs before the fire in his club, and lit his cigar, 'that the offence of malicious damage can't be extended to the hurt people do to each other in their emotional lives.'

Lord Sennowe snorted but said nothing.

'Look at that poor girl in court today,' the judge went on. 'You were as responsible as anyone for her finding herself in that predicament.' Lord Sennowe stared into the vermilion depths of his glass, his mind full of memories.

'You're quite wrong, Bertie,' he said after a pause. 'That comes under an entirely different heading. It's called *delicious* damage, and it is, thank God, entirely beyond the reach of the law.'

'In my view,' said the judge, totally ignoring his friend's remark, 'today saw a grave miscarriage of justice.'

'How so?'

'Well – I summed up as fairly as I could, but definitely with an acquittal in mind. After all, Chesterfield knew of La Metternich. No-one disputed that her formidable reputation went before her. We saw how she was dressed . . .'

'Hold on!' interrupted his friend. 'I can't believe you're really sitting there and saying that her clothes deprived her of the protection of the law. We heard that ghastly evidence about her cries. What could have been plainer?'

'Oh yes.' The old judge smiled, a thin line of yellowed teeth revealed between his withered lips. 'Certainly that was why he was convicted. Despite my very plain explanation to the contrary, couched, I like to think, in the most limpid English, a language as familiar as Sanskrit to the average juror nowadays, the jury chose to see it as a contest between Chesterfield and your young woman.'

'Wasn't it?'

'Of course not. That wasn't the issue before the jury at all. The Law states that a man is innocent unless proved guilty beyond a reasonable doubt. In my humble opinion,' he sniffed and drew on his cigar, the very picture of exaggerated and false humility, 'there was a reasonable doubt. Very reasonable indeed, notwithstanding that harpy changing her evidence in the middle of the case. I had supposed that was why they were out for so long. In my simplicity, I had assumed it was to make him sweat before letting him off.'

'So why such a stiff sentence?'

'Aha! Oh . . . er . . . Simpkins?' The judge raised a languid hand to a passing steward. 'His lordship would like another glass of this port, please. And so would I.' The steward smiled and hurried away. 'I had no choice. As far as the general public are concerned, he was unanimously found guilty of a serious offence. A light sentence would have proclaimed that the so-called "Establishment" was looking after its own.'

'So poor Charles has to suffer the injustice of a long sentence for a crime you don't think he committed simply to spare your blushes?'

'*Pro bono publico*, old boy,' drawled the Judge. '*Pro bono publico!* Mind you,' he added, 'oh, thank you, Simpkins.' He waited until the club servant had left the room. 'I have had a quiet word already with Bob Trefusis at the Home Office. I don't doubt that Chesterfield will go straight to an open prison, and maybe he'll find himself out on licence rather sooner than usual if we can avoid press comment. After all, at the very worst, he'll get parole in a little over two years, but a deterioration of health, a doctor who knows the ropes . . . who knows . . . nine months? He was with my brother at school, you know. Nine months at Ford is a damn sight lighter than five years in Common Lane!'

Lord Sennowe leant back in his chair and closed his eyes. What an extraordinary career his casual infatuated suggestion had opened up for Perky in his frosted garden, all those years ago. He could even remember the sprightly tune the band had been playing, and the moonlight touching her breasts with silver. She had been so young. I wish . . . but his thoughts petered away among the fumes of the port. Shaking his head, he drained his glass, and waving a silent salute to the judge, who was already half dozing, he crossed the hall to get his raincoat and walked down into the damp street to find his chauffeur.

'Home, m'lord?' The driver, a patient man from the fens, had been thinking wistfully of his wife, alone in their little cottage at the gates of his employer's park. With luck, they could be the right side of Norwich by midnight.

'Good heavens, no!' the older man replied, laughing. 'Annabel's. I need cheering up.'

The last of the year's roses were just beginning to blossom when the church bells at Milston pealed out across the valley to celebrate the marriage of Laura Ingram, spinster of the parish, to Timothy Bryce, bachelor, of the parish of St James the Ineluctable, Chelsea.

Max and Flora had returned from Siena for the occasion, and he, looking bronzed and slightly dangerous, led Laura up the aisle, while Flora perched herself inconspicuously at the back of the side aisle, between Mrs Stubbs and Mr Gregory. If the old barrister recognized her, he gave no sign of it, moving up the pew to make room for the creamy flounces of her new dress. Laura's mother, unusually chic in eau-de-nil, welcomed her errant husband beside her with a warm forgiving smile. It was, she knew, the reaction that would most annoy him.

Behind them sat squabbling ranks of Ingrams, a massive presence of Woodchesters, and assorted friends from London. On the other side, a plump homely woman, incongruously swathed in tartan, showed that Tim's mother had decided to cross the Atlantic to rediscover her son. Perky and Dapper were in the second row behind her, self-conscious objects of intense interest to those across the aisle who knew their respective histories. To their great regret, her fabled jewellery was not in evidence. Only the slender gold band of her wedding ring disturbed the pale perfection of her skin.

Now the bellringers, Stubbs and Bob, supervising four younger men, set to, to publish the successful completion of the ceremony with their intricate pattern of sound. Laura, pausing on the steps beside Tim, as the bridesmaids clustered round her ready for the photographers, caught a flash of red in the corner of the graveyard.

There were fresh geraniums on a recent grave. Ironically, it had been Mrs Stubbs who had died suddenly during the winter, the sudden victim of a massive stroke. Laura turned to Tim, who instinctively kissed her.

'That's it! Do it again, squire!'

The photographers, professional and amateur, shouted encouragement over the frantic metallic sounds of their trade.

'I love you,' she whispered.

'What?' He bent down again. 'I can't hear for all this din.'

'I LOVE YOU!' The sudden silencing of the bells coincided with her exasperated shout.

'That's right, Miss!' shouted one of the villagers. 'You give him a piece of your mind.'

And amid general applause, he kissed her again.

THE END

THE BRIDGWATER SALE

Freddie Stockdale

'AN AFFECTIONATE PICTURE OF ENGLISH COUNTRY,
"COUNTY" LIFE . . . I ENJOYED IT VERY MUCH INDEED'
Jessica Mann, *Sunday Telegraph*

John Griffin is in love with the company ceramics expert, tall, slender, desirable-but-married Mary. Mary loves Terry, the Chairman's sidekick, and so does Lionel, heir to the Bridgwater millions. Terry loves only himself.

John runs the Berington branch of Merrywethers, one of the top three art auction houses in the country. But as the market falls, and the competition gets fiercer, is he really tough enough, nasty enough, for the job? Does he pursue the dead and dying with sufficient tenacity to bring their business to Merrywethers? Terry thinks not; and Terry has the Chairman's ear.

As blackmail, forgery, fraud and sexual enticement darken the atmosphere, and as John and Terry fight it out both at work and over Mary, *The Bridgwater Sale* explores the cut-throat and glamorous world of art auction sales with a sparkling wit.

'A WITTY AND WELL-SHAPED PLOT LEADS US INTO THE LIGHTEST OF COMEDIES. A TOP-CLASS DEBUT'
David Hughes, *Mail on Sunday*

'STOCKDALE INJECTS A WRY HUMOUR INTO THE OFTEN QUESTIONABLE PROCEEDINGS AND IS A MASTER OF CREATING BOTH HILARIOUS AND PAINFULLY EMBARRASSING SITUATIONS'
Gloucestershire Echo

0 552 99546 0

BLACK SWAN

A SELECTION OF FINE WRITING
AVAILABLE FROM BLACK SWAN

THE PRICES SHOWN BELOW WERE CORRECT AT THE TIME OF GOING TO PRESS. HOWEVER TRANSWORLD PUBLISHERS RESERVE THE RIGHT TO SHOW NEW RETAIL PRICES ON COVERS WHICH MAY DIFFER FROM THOSE PREVIOUSLY ADVERTISED IN THE TEXT OR ELSEWHERE.

☐	99550 9	**THE FAME HOTEL**	*Terence Blacker*	£5.99
☐	99531 2	**AFTER THE HOLE**	*Guy Burt*	£5.99
☐	99524 X	**YANKING UP THE YO-YO**	*Michael Carson*	£5.99
☐	99466 9	**A SMOKING DOT IN THE DISTANCE**	*Ivor Gould*	£6.99
☐	99609 2	**FORREST GUMP**	*Winston Groom*	£5.99
☐	99169 4	**GOD KNOWS**	*Joseph Heller*	£7.99
☐	99538 X	**GOOD AS GOLD**	*Joseph Heller*	£6.99
☐	99208 9	**THE 158LB MARRIAGE**	*John Irving*	£5.99
☐	99204 6	**THE CIDER HOUSE RULES**	*John Irving*	£6.99
☐	99567 3	**SAILOR SONG**	*Ken Kesey*	£6.99
☐	99542 8	**SWEET THAMES**	*Matthew Kneale*	£6.99
☐	99595 9	**LITTLE FOLLIES**	*Eric Kraft*	£5.99
☐	99569 X	**MAYBE THE MOON**	*Armistead Maupin*	£5.99
☐	99461 8	**THE DEATH OF DAVID DEBRIZZI**	*Paul Micou*	£5.99
☐	99597 5	**COYOTE BLUE**	*Christopher Moore*	£5.99
☐	99577 0	**THE CONFESSIONS OF AUBREY BEARDSLEY**	*Donald S. Olson*	£7.99
☐	99536 3	**IN THE PLACE OF FALLEN LEAVES**	*Tim Pears*	£5.99
☐	99551 7	**SUFFER THE LITTLE CHILDREN**	*Lucy Robertson*	£5.99
☐	99122 8	**THE HOUSE OF GOD**	*Samuel Shem*	£6.99
☐	99540 1	**ITS COLOURS THEY ARE FINE**	*Alan Spence*	£5.99
☐	99546 0	**THE BRIDGWATER SALE**	*Freddie Stockdale*	£5.99
☐	99130 9	**NOAH'S ARK**	*Barbara Trapido*	£6.99
☐	99056 6	**BROTHER OF THE MORE FAMOUS JACK**	*Barbara Trapido*	£6.99
☐	99495 2	**A DUBIOUS LEGACY**	*Mary Wesley*	£6.99
☐	99591 6	**A MISLAID MAGIC**	*Joyce Windsor*	£4.99
☐	99500 2	**THE RUINS OF TIME**	*Ben Woolfenden*	£4.99